monkey

by
frank mosco

A division of Quillquest Enterprises.

Quillquest Books, Quillquest Junior Books, Quillquest Classic Books
and the sailing quill are the exclusive trademarks of Quillquest Enterprises.
For information or to comment about this book contact
Quillquestbooks@msn.com

Hardback edition
ISBN 0-9769272-9-2 Quillquest Books, 2006

Paperback edition
ISBN 0-9769272-2-5 Quillquest Books, 2005

for

My Breahmonkey
May you never lose your wonderful imagination.

monkey

by

frank mosco

Quillquest Books
USA

note from the author

In the early 1930s Hollywood produced an epic movie about a great gorilla known as KONG, a movie that elevated the American people's imaginations and cinematic expectations to a new and higher plain. That movie lives on to this day as a benchmark moment in entertainment history as well as a long accepted part of our culture. Yet there are few people who know the true story and inspiration behind that great epic and even fewer who can relate the actual facts about the beast and the mysterious island on which it existed.

Within the pages of this book you will discover the truth regarding what is now considered to be one of the greatest myths of all time, a truth that goes far beyond pop culture, the glitter and search lights of Hollywood, and all the speculation of lesser men. How I came by this story is unimportant. What is important is that you understand what lies on these pages is a revelation so incredible it could never have been imagined or invented.

"This is that story - and I'm stickin' to it."

chapter 1

They sat there, hundreds of them, there in the dark like dumfounded mushrooms, flinching with every strident scream and cringing with every reverberating roar. The two frightening sounds, one of fear and terror, the other a threatening primordial horror emanated from an unimaginable sight, both coming together and echoing throughout the large dark room to be seared permanently into the psyche of all those present. Sounds so imposing and unnerving and unforgettable they would become famously recognized and fear provoking all around the world.

"Oh God!" Whispered a woman, looking about at the others as she reached and took her husband's arm for security.

The chilling sounds washed over them like the cold wind of a nor'easter storm yet resulted in an agitating hot sweat of expectation and fear. It was like nothing they had ever experienced, nothing they had ever read, ever imagined or ever dreamt. Nothing.

They all sat there, wide-eyed, looking up at something horrible, bigger than life, seeing it for the first time and they were terrified, consternated.

Another bone chilling ROAR!

Another blood curdling SCREAM!

The flickering light played off their blanched faces and their mouths fell open and dry in astonishment. They squirmed in their seats, feet shuffling, palms sweating, wanting to turn away but for some reason remaining reluctantly fixed on the spectacle in front of them.

"Oh my God," the woman whispered nervously, still clenching the arm of her husband.

The thing was there now, in front of her, in front of all of them, above them, frightening, larger than life and larger still again.

"Oh my God!" she repeated with a slight tremble, nearly coming to tears.

The thing had arrived for all mankind to see, crashing from its world to ours, unconstrained and threatening, towering above all civilized reality without shame, without conscience and without fear, totally without fear.

"SCREAM!"

"ROAR!"

"SCREAM!"

A small boy curled back into his seat, peeking through his fingers. Next to him sat his little sister, intensely frightened, scared, not just scared but scared senseless with her face buried, hidden in her brother's shoulder as she jumped and twitched with each shattering scream and roar. She wanted it to go away, to just go away.

Outside, away from this impending horror, night had already fallen and a dull fog had engulfed the Hudson River and the harbor. Across the river the canyons of 1933 New York were only discernible by the many lights of her towering buildings and other mammoth monuments of progress. High above, the city was topped by a gray reflection off an umbrella of lingering haze created by the heat of life which emanated from the creatures and traffic below. Cars and cabs scurried up and down the avenues, their engines and horns echoing off the urban walls and windows.

Out there people shuffled along the sidewalks, oblivious of the monstrous revelation taking place in their midst, in that large dark room where hundreds of their fellow citizens were losing their cinematic innocence. Losing it by watching for the first time the biggest, baddest damn monster ever conceived. Where they watched and came to fear... Kong, King Kong, the great ape. Where they saw Kong crashing through the jungle to discover the love of his life, Fay Ray. Where Kong, the great natural mystery and the proclaimed eighth wonder of the world was now crashing through the massive heavy gates of a huge ancient wall and into a native village, destroying, ravaging, killing, snatching and actually eating fleeing natives. Kong would do all this and more for he was seriously pissed off, pissed off at the entire world just because some damn sailor stole his little woman.

Among the hundreds of spellbound people in the audience sat two young men, one Bartholomew "Bart" Haile and one Stanley Corbit Wellington III. Bart had easily become wide-eyed and terrified like the rest of the audience in the theater. In fact he was so damn nervous he was even smiling. Stanley Wellington however was more rational. He knew it was simply another Hollywood flick and he wasn't about to be sucked into a pseudo psychological moment of anxiety. Always composed, that was Stanley, cool, calm and collected not to mention stinking rich and handsome. Bart on the other hand, well, Bart was Bart and no one else. He wore his heart on his sleeve and his tie in his pocket, a real potluck stew of emotions and more often than not was too honest and outspoken for his own good.

When the movie drew to its conclusion Kong, the great gorilla, had caused all kinds of mayhem in Manhattan and was now right in up-town New York high atop the tallest building in the world. Kong had taken the beautiful girl and taken the Empire State Building and he was seriously pissed off... again. Pissed off this time because airplanes were spitting bullets at him and his elusive lady.

"Scream!"

"Roar!"

Rat tat tat tat tat tat.

It seemed our killer Kong just couldn't get any respect, typical New York, so he reached out and snatched one of those damn pesky bullet spraying biplanes with one hand and tossed it away like a bad banana. Bart stared at the screen awestruck, amazed, then afforded himself a quick glance at his friend, discovering to his astonishment that Stanley appeared to be almost bored. When he looked back to the big screen Kong had finally been conquered by the planes, falling to the streets far far below where he was quickly surrounded by the curious citizens of Gothem. Jack Armstrong, playing Carl Denham, Kong's captor, made his way through the crowd to deliver an historic eulogy.

"Well Denham, the planes got him," observed a nearby constable.

"Oh no. Wasn't the planes that got him," replied Denham. "It was beauty killed the beast."

Yeah right.

And so there it ended as the music rose and hundreds of hearts in the theater fell. The great terrifying Kong had become just another poor slob who drew the short straw in just another Hollywood love triangle. Yep, that beauty will get you every time just like Kong, relegated to the likes of Bogart and Valentino. For a relieved audience however, justice and humanity had once again prevailed, reinforcing their belief that there is no beast or force on earth, no matter how great, which could conquer the City of New York. Not today. Not in 1933. Not ever. At least that's what they thought.

When the theater patrons exited the building, the space and light and reality of the street as well as the crisp air of late fall offered a welcomed relief from the frightening confines of the great gorilla Kong experience. Thelma, the highly agitated woman who nearly squeezed the blood from her husband's arm during the movie, was more than relieved to be away from the big screen horror. However she continued holding his arm for comfort and support as they made their way through the crowd. When a taxi pulled to the curb her husband was helping her on with her coat and while doing so observed her uneasy glances to the heights of the Empire State Building.

"Oh really now, Thelma. Be serious," he chided. "After all, it was only a movie."

"Only a movie," she repeated, hoping her expressed repetition would be reassuring but it wasn't. "Only a movie."

He opened the door to the taxi and helped her in. As he donned his hat before entering behind her he too turned and glanced up at the towering skyscraper. A brief chill ran up his spine and he wondered if it were indeed possible. When he entered the cab the high-strung Thelma stated apprehensively, "I could use a drink. I could really use a drink. Now."

"Well, my dear, if you insist," he readily agreed.

Just as the cab pulled away Stanley and Bart exited the theater. They could easily be taken for what they were, a pair of ivy leaguers, evident by their appearance, age and demeanor. Stanley, the most handsome, was much better dressed, afforded to him by vast sums of money and enterprise acquired by four generations of successful Wellingtons. Bart, to the contrary, was a bit less refined, wearing a letterman's sweater and worn corduroy slacks under a well seasoned coat with a near homely mismatched but much loved and appreciated scarf made by his grandmother. If he was at all disadvantaged in looks or otherwise as compared to his friend Stanley, it didn't trouble him in the least for he was never one to be concerned about social impressions or status. He sported a full head of blond hair, a fair share of freckles and a wonderful broad shit-eating smile and disposition that few people could resist. Simply stated, Bart Haile was an agreeable piece of work in spite of himself.

"Well, that was an interesting distraction," observed Stanley.   "Distraction? Distraction? Hell, Stanley, any more distractions like that and I'm gonna' need therapy. Didn't you see that thing or were you sleeping through the entire show? And that Fay Wray... wooooh, hey, what a dish, huh?   What I wouldn't give to be that monkey for a day. Just one day on an island with her and I would…"

Stanley laughed as he pulled a cigarette from a gold case, stuck it in a silver holder, clamped it between his teeth and popped a match on his fingernail to light up.

"Listen Bart old man," he said as he started to light his cigarette. "We're law students, future levelheaded guardians of fortune and industry. We can't allow ourselves to be emotionally shaken by the antics of a fictitious Hollywood monkey."

Before Stanley could bring the match to meet the cigarette his wrist was gripped and stayed firmly by the rough strong hand of a stranger.

"Monkey?" said the stranger.

Stanley turned to discover an old sailor in an aged wool p-coat and a seaman's cap. The old sailor pulled the burning match to his pipe, drew heavily until the pipe was well lit and then released Stanley's wrist. The flaring light of the match revealed the leathery aged face of a hard lived and long traveled old man with an imposing scar that crossed through his left eyebrow down to his upper cheek.

"Monkey? Fictitious?" he grunted as he drew on his pipe. "What the hell do you know? Thanks for the light kid," he concluded as he turned and walked away, favoring his left leg with an obvious limp.

"And I suppose you're an expert?" said Stanley, tossing the match.

The old sailor paused and turned, "On monkeys, hell no. Couldn't rightly give a damn," he said; then returned to settle close to Bart and Stanley. "But that creature in there…" He near whispered with a nervous chuckle, then looking about, uneasy. "I been places. Seen things.

Things you can't imagine. I knows the truth, boy," he looked over his shoulder at the theater marquee. "Not that movie shit in there. It's the truth I be know'n, I say."

Bart was immediately fascinated by the mystery of the old man. Stanley remained characteristically indifferent. The old sailor detected Stanley's doubt and dismissed and shunned him with a grunt and a wave then turned and walked away.

"Crazy old man," Stanley mumbled.

"Stanley my good fellow, where's your sense of curiosity," smiled Bart as he perked up and patted Stanley on the back. "Besides, what the hell else have we got to do?"

Bart quickly caught up to the old sailor while Stanley stood, struck another match and lit his cigarette. He watched as Bart appeared to reach some sort of agreement with the stranger and when they returned together he simply shook his head thinking he was about to become the victim of another of Bart's nonsensical high jinks.

"Stanley, I think we would do well to listen to our new-found friend here. As dear grandma Haile always said, 'Taking in an old man's wisdom is far more enlightening than reading all the books ever written by unlived savants'."

"Right. Your grandmother said that?"

"Yeah well, actually it was more like, 'Shut the hell up and listen to your grandfather or I'll slap you,' but does that make it any less relevant?."

Bart took both men by the arm and escorted them along the street. "Gentlemen, what say we take some sustenance and talk awhile? Chew the fat as they say back on the farm."

"You didn't grow up on a farm," observed Stanley. "You're from Flatbush."

"Yeah, but I have an agricultural heritage."

"Bart, your father was a dentist and your grandfather was a barber."

"Damn it Stanley, you're always splitting hairs."

chapter 2

A short time later the three men found themselves sitting in the booth of a nearby diner with the old sailor shoveling down his second helping of the blue plate special. He motioned to a passing waitress for more coffee. Stanley sat bored as he watched the young lady fill the old man's cup. When he looked to Bart who was thoroughly enjoying the sight of this hungry man filling his needs, he could hold himself silent no longer.

"Bart, I thought we were here to relish the wisdom of an old…"

"Hard times, sonny," interrupted the old sailor. "Gotta' gets whatcha' can when ya can. Depression on, ya know. World's gone and got a little crazy. Things don't come easy no more."

Stanley leaned back, unimpressed, "Yeah, well…"

"So my friend, about this monkey?" Bart asked of their opportunist guest.

The old sailor paused seriously, a mouth full of food. He studied Bart's eyes then looked to Stanley and back again to Bart.

"Monkey?" he said through his food then swallowed. "Monkey's a little furry critter ya gives a French whore for a good time and some laughs, sonny. Nope, ain't no monkey yarn I can tell. More'n that. Much more. Ain't nothin' like you can possibly imagine. Ain't fit for words… or the ears of decent folk."

"Yeah well, we aren't decent folk," smiled Bart. "We're future lawyers."

The old sailor grunted, sat back and pulled out his pipe. He looked expectantly at Stanley who pulled a match out of his pocket and tossed it across the table.

"College boys, eh,' said the old seaman as he packed and lit his pipe and studied the two young men. He tossed the spent match on the now empty plate where it sizzled out in the remaining gravy.

"So you just played us for a free meal, eh pops?" asked Stanley.

The old man shot a look of displeasure at the well-healed upper class Ivy Leaguer but quickly subdued it.

"Well, ya see… ain't never told nobody before. Ain't never wanted to. But them dumb-ass picture show shit heads…" He took a generous gulp of his coffee and continued, "Them shit heads got it all wrong. Way off course," he said, then noticing a trembling in his hand, set down the coffee. The old sailor looked to his pipe to discover his other hand trembling as well. "I ain't got much more time in this world. Ain't got no family I know of."

He rose from the booth, put on his p-coat and cap and started for the door.

Stanley threw up his hands and looked to Bart, "Told you it was a waste of time."

"Maybe he's shy," suggested Bart.

"Yeah, like a fox."

Just then the old sailor turned back and motioned for Bart and Stanley to join him, "Ahoy there."

Bart jumped up with a smile joined reluctantly by Stanley who dug in his pocket and tossed some money on the table. As they departed, Bart looked to Stanley mouthing to himself jokingly, "Ahoy there?".

The fog engulfed the cold harbor limiting the vision along the docks and wharf area and offering only a partial view of the large hulking rusty steamers straining at their thick heavy mooring lines. They sat tied in the damp misty shadows of the long dark wharf like so many ghost ships, each with only a few dim lights acknowledging their presence. A ship's bell sounded in harmony with a distant foghorn and the occasional blustering of intoxicated sailors and longshoremen drifted from a nearby bar. The old sailor, Bart and Stanley had just emerged from the fog along the dock when their attention was drawn to the sound of a breaking bottle and they turned to observe a drunken young merchant seaman stumble, fall and pass out against a netted pile of cargo. Unaware of their presence, a bum slithered out of the nearby shadows to take advantage of the young mariner's unfortunate state and hastily began picking through his pockets. Stanley moved to stop the theft but to his surprise he was restrained by the old sailor.

"Belay that mate. He's a young'n," explained the old man. "If that thieving feller pulls a blade we'll lend a hand for sure but that young seaman's gotta learn his lesson. Better he lose a little coin now and earn him some wisdom or next time around it won't be just his purse he might be givin' up."

The three of them watched as the bum snatched the seaman's money and ran off into the darkness then they continued walking along the wharf until the old sailor found a suitable spot allotting him a view past the moored ships. He could see nothing but fog yet as he sat heavily on a crate near an unloaded stack of cargo he looked into the distance with interest, possibly seeing a world yet to be traveled or remembering one which had. Stanley surveyed the surrounding wharf with suspicion, thinking the old man may have drawn them into something ominous. Bart wandered about and childishly stretched over the bulkhead, squinting down into the dark dirty water. Something nearby drew his attention and he looked to discover an extremely large wharf rat, easily the size of a husky cat, scurrying up a thick ship's mooring line.

"Big," shivered Bart. "Biggest damn mouse I ever saw."

"They say the fog is the restless souls of sailors lost to the sea and if you listen close, real close mind you, you can hear 'em callin' ya to join 'em."

The two young men looked out into the dense fog blanketing the harbor then Stanley turned his attention back to the dark passages of the docks.

"It was back in eighty-nine," continued the old sailor. "I missed the war. Too young."

Bart turned to the old man, "The great war? With the Kaiser?"

"Eighty-nine, sonny. War between the states. I comes off the farm outa' Ohio back in seventy-one. Went to be a whaler but the whalin' was died off so's I worked the merchant cargo ships to Europe and then shipped out west to Asia and the China trade. That's where the story begins. Eighty-nine, in Borneo."

"Borneo?"

"Yep. Was workin' the Saint Jane, a big four-master outa' San Francisco. Now she was a real sweet lady that Saint Jane but a real serious job of concern she was too. We catched us an unfortunate storm outa' New Guinea, the southern end of a deviate typhoon, and had to put into Borneo for repairs."

Stanley lit a cigarette and relaxed against the pile of crates in anticipation of what he expected to be the old man's lengthy cock-and-bull story.

"Yep, Borneo. We had us some time on our hands ya see 'cause the First Mate he got sick and the Capt'n had to wait for a doctor. Anyways, a couple of us boys got a little rumbustuous. You know, too much rum and some unsavory ladies."

Bart looked to Stanley and smiled. He was taking a liking to the old man and sat next to him so as not to miss any part of what he thought was becoming a colorful sea tale of interest.

"Anyways, we all ends up in some local pig pen them Borneo heathens called a jail where we comes across this old Samoan. Tattooed head to toe, he was. If ya hadn't known better ya'd s'pect he had a shrunk head in every pocket and designs on yer own. Well, turns out this old man was in dire health and short ta live, wantin' nothin' more but to ease his pain. So we take him out, gives him the last of our rum to kill his ailin' and in his gratitude just afore he died, he offers up a story… and a map."

"A map," echoed Bart.

"Sure 'nuff," said the old sailor as he tapped the spent tobacco out of his pipe on the side of the crate and watched as the ashes fell to the ground.

"Map... changed my life, it did," he continued. "Changed all our lives." He packed in some fresh tobacco from an old leather pouch. "Them that lived, that is."

"Changed. How?" asked a now interested Stanley.

"Don't get me wrong, now. It weren't no mutiny or

nothin'," said the old man, looking down in shame. "Not to speak of."

"What do you mean?" asked Bart.

"Well ya see, right after we put to sea the Capt'n up and died. Just up and died. And we'd left the First Officer in Borneo. Heard later he died same as the Capt'n. Bad food or some damn shit like that. So's there we was kinda' rudderless and we had this map. Map was wrote in Portaguee it was but we had this ship's carpenter could read Portaguee. Turns out this map was about an uncharted island in the Indian Ocean below the 'quator somewhere's 'tween Sumatra and Madagascar... with riches. Not your usual storybook treasure kind of tripe mind you but riches, untapped. Mountain full of diamonds there just for the pickin' just like that Samoan said, but..." He paused while digging through his pockets to come up with a match. Finding one he struck it on his shoe, lit and drew on his pipe and continued, "...seems all them few souls fortunate 'nuff to find them diamonds never lived long 'nuff... ta..."

"Never lived. Why?" asked Stanley.

"Island was... s'posed to be cursed. Protected... by..." The old sailor squirmed, growing nervous with the troubling memories flashing through his mind.

"What?" urged Bart.

"Beast... a... god-awful beast," replied the old sailor, raising his pipe to his mouth only to discover it was extinguished. His hand was shaking. Stanley struck a match and held it for him.

"A beast?" asked Stanley, noticing the old man's quick recovery with just a few puffs of the pipe and wondering what kind of exotic tobacco could be so soothing.

"So anyways, the crew took a vote," the sailor continued."Decided to venture out for them diamonds, we did. Had nothin' to lose, you see. With no capt'n it weren't likely we'd be makin' much coin for our efforts of takin' the Saint Jane home right off. Ship's owners weren't too generous back then, ya know. Most likely would of accused us of some kind of conspiratorial shenanigans. Maybe even hung us."

"You went there? To the island?" asked Bart.

"We went. Better we'd gone straight to hell I say." He fell silent as he removed his hat and set it on the crate beside him then wiped his brow with a kerchief.

After a moment Stanley stood tall, stretched, checked his watch and nodded to Bart, "Getting late. We have a match tomorrow."

Bart nodded agreement then turned to the old sailor. "Did you find the diamonds?" he asked as he rose to depart.

"What we found..." replied the old man nervously. "What we found no man should ever see."

He sat back relishing his pipe, remembering.

Stanley looked to Bart with a shrug, thinking he had run out of story, then the old mariner continued.

"Diamonds? Yes sir, you can sure ring that to be true. Big as your fist they was, plump as a Dutch mama. And plentiful to. Solomon himself can't imagine. Sure, we found 'em... but that weren't all we found."

The old sailor fell silent once again as he gazed into the fog and drifted into the past, seemingly not to return. After a long moment Stanley drew some cash from his pocket and set it easily into the old man's hat. As an afterthought he tossed in his matches then turned and walked off.

"Take care old man," said Bart as he patted him on the back and walked away. "It was a grand yarn. Enjoyed it."

"Wait!" called out the old sailor, causing Bart and Stanley to stop and turn. "You don't understand. I was the only one... The whole ship's company and the only one to live. Never told nobody... till now." He retrieved his hat, rose and walked to the boys then reached into his coat withdrawing an aged canvas pouch and held it to his chest.

"It's alright old man," said Bart. You don't have to explain. We understand."

He extended the pouch to Bart.

"Really, it's quite alright," Bart added. "You don't owe us anything."

"Do you read Portaguee?" asked the old sailor seriously, handing the pouch to Bart..

"What... You mean... The map?" came Bart as he accepted it.

"Some souls might say it's a map," offered the old man. "I'd say it's... a doomed course to perdition."

Bart unwrapped the old canvas to discover a yellow aged folded piece of parchment. It was indeed a map and while Bart and Stanley turned and inspected it in the dim limited light of a nearby ship the old sailor silently turned and walked away, quickly disappearing into the misty shadows. When the boys turned back they discovered they were alone.

"Gone. He's gone."

"I didn't catch his name," said Stanley.

"He wouldn't tell me his name and didn't want mine. Said he was a man of the sea and too many names hindered his passage."

The seasoned sailor stooped a bit as he favored and rubbed the old injury in his leg. As he limped through the heavy mist a distant foghorn sang through the harbor and he paused, turned to the lingering sound, struck a match and relit his pipe. By the brief glow of the match came visible his haggard face as it grew a sly devious smile.

chapter 3

It was old money, grandiose, impressive, imposing, ostentatious, and expansive, as it was designed and intended to be. Just another run of the mill Hudson Valley granite mansion, its origins dating back to the feudal landlord days prior to the American Revolution. Even in the dark of the evening it conveyed old world opulence seemingly for no reason other than to stand its occupants above most others. An opulence of which could be seen at all turns of its architectural character.

Each of the many rooms behind every ornate window was softly lit, demonstrating the grand house was fully alive on this evening. Likewise each window had only a single candle, a decorative Christmas holiday understatement as much as the made to order limited yet seasonally beautiful snow. From within the mansion could be heard a string quartet playing holiday classics yet still, in another place and time with a different moon and mist, one could swear some country club Count Dracula could comfortably call this home.

A well-suited middle-aged Irish doorman stood outside the main entrance and greeted the many guests as they arrived. His breath danced in a cloud of steam as he patted his gloves and shifted his feet to combat the cold. He was freezing his ass off but his Irish pride prevented him from revealing this to the arriving guest. Consequently after each affluent clan entered the mansion he would pull out a flask, hold it high and offer up a poetic toast.

"As I stand here so bold, so bold in the cold, servin' the lord of the manor. I take comfort in knowin' and I'll never be showin' that me balls have yet dropped with a clamor," composed the doorman prior to taking another heavy swig.

To the expressed delight of the doorman the fine warming Irish whisky served its purpose.

"Ahhh, sheer poetry it is," he said as he capped the flask then addressed it as though it were his own mother. "Thank you me darlin'. It's more comfort ya bring than the Pope's own blessin'."

The flask was quickly stashed in his coat with the arrival of still another limousine full of guests to attend the celebrated annual Wellington Christmas Gala. He opened the vehicle door and out flowed the formally clad socialites, passing him as though he were just another shrub growing near the Wellington's immaculate stone entrance walkway. They then filtered into the mansion and the main ballroom, emerging into a sparkling and colorful privileged setting far removed from the reality of the depression that now gripped the outside world.

In the room's center stood an impressively tall Christmas tree decorated to the hilt with gold and silver heirloom ornaments, ribbons, fruits, small candles, and more. The guests flowed and mingled among themselves, ranging in carriage and appearance from perfectly beautiful and perfectly mannered to down right eloquently obnoxious, with the measure of most seemingly dependant on whether their jewelry gained as much notice as the Wellington holiday tree. They talked, smiled, drifted along, smiled, sipped, smiled some more and basically tried to impress each other, all the while politely and secretly critically analyzing and evaluating each other, not as friends and neighbors but as rivals and competitors. Then there, like a toad in a rose garden, amidst all this pomp and intentional happenstance, appeared an alien shit-eating smile in the form of Bart Haile wondering about uncomfortably in a borrowed tuxedo. One of the Wellington servants who appeared better dressed and tailored than Bart, approached with a tray of champagne but for some reason after sizing up our boy decided to blow on by.

"Um, excuse me," called Bart, noticing the servant's intentional disregard and passing.

The servant stopped, offering Bart only a supercilious half smile.

"Is that champagne you have there?" inquired Bart.

The servant afforded a slight nod yes and unenthusiastically offered, "Would you care for a glass... sir?"

"Nope, never drink the shit. I hear it induces impotence."

The servant remained unimpressed, "Would you prefer a... Christmas punch... sir?"

"Only if I get to throw the first one," smiled Bart.

"Yes sir," replied the still unimpressed snobby servant as he turned away. Bart had been bested by the help, he thought. Or had he?

"A fool who would be king," Bart tossed out in Latin to the departing arrogant servant.

"An ass who would be a fool," replied the servant. In Latin.

"Touché," Bart mumbled to himself, turning away in defeat. "The son-of-a-bitch got me."

His dejection lasted but only moments however, nipped in the bud when he spied an exceptionally attractive and appealing debutante standing alone near the punch bowl.

Bart restored his broad smile and slid across the room for the kill. The debutante scarcely noticed his arrival.

"Wonderful evening isn't it?" Bart offered as an icebreaker.

The lovely girl stood poised, offering no response.

"May I pour you a glass of punch?" offered Bart.

Again the young socialite beauty stood ignorant of his presence. Bart, having taken the hint and refusing to go down without swinging asked, "So my dear, just how long have you had this affliction anyway?"

The girl suddenly came alive, gasping, insulted. "Well I never…" she said as she hustled across the room, taking refuge with a nearby clan of peacockish old hens. "Such a creature," she told them. "The Wellingtons should be more selective about whom they employ for these occasions."

Bart stood by the punch bowl, rejected. He inspected and adjusted his ill-fitting tuxedo, cupped his hand and sampled his breath.

"The Red Baron strikes again, eh old man?" observed Stanley as he glided up and put his arm around Bart's shoulders. "Don't take it to heart," he continued. "She's been conditioned. She'll marry for money, copulate out of necessity and die a dried up old hag."

"What a waste," observed Bart.

"Hmm," agreed Stanley as he drew Bart away. "This valley is full of Victorian holdovers. It's as though the twenties passed them by altogether. It's damn depressing some times."

They strolled through the maze of low-key socialites, offering nods and smiles as they talked.

"I'm in need of your services, old man," said Stanley.

"You? In need of anything? Get serious."

"I'm to join my father in the library for my annual

recapitulation and flogging. I could use your moral support."

"I'm afraid my morals wouldn't impress your father very much."

"A free cigar and brandy," offered Stanley.

"You S O B. You think I can be bought cheap don't you? Just because I'm going to become a lawyer."

"Actually I didn't think of it that way but now that you mention it…"

"Okay, you drive a hard bargain," surrendered Bart. "But I refuse to defend your torrid affair with that voluptuous Turkish belly dancer in Toledo. I have my standards you know."

"Bart, that wasn't me in Toledo. It was you."

"No no, I remember… Oh yeah. Right. You were with the Romanian stripper in Philadelphia. Now that was torrid. Absolutely disgusting. She had a mustache."

"No, the belly dancer had the mustache. Philadelphia was the beautiful Norwegian ballet dancer. The Ambassador's daughter."

"Well, just the same, I'm not defending any of your damn disgusting adventuresome affairs no matter where the hell they happened."

"That's fine, Bart. You won't be expected to. I only need you to help me fend off the beast."

"Beast. What beast?"

"The beast of tradition and drudgery. The Wellington ball and chain of heredity."

"I have no damn idea what the hell you're talking

about, my friend," smiled Bart. "But okay, let's go slay the beast."

Of course the library of the Wellington mansion was impressive, inclusive of walnut paneling, a vaulted ceiling, portraits of unrecognizable famous men, models of famous ships that contributed to the acquisition of the Wellington fortune, and more books than any civilized person should ever read for fear of inducing an intellectual coma. And into this den of opulent heritage, through stately hand carved double doors, entered Stanley and Bart who were met and greeted by a sophisticated, pragmatic father, one Stanley Corbit Wellington II, himself.

"Ah, boys. Come in, come in," he greeted as he led them to a setting of fine liquors in cut crystal. "Brandy? Cigar?"

It wasn't so much an offer but more a suggestion not to be refused. He poured a brandy and handed the glass to Bart.

"Mr. Bartholomew Haile. Correct?"

"Correct, sir," smiled Bart.

"I never forget a name or a face. That's paramount to men of our ilk. You'd be wise to remember that, Mr. Haile," said Wellington II.

"I'll certainly do that, um… Mr. um…"

"Wellington."

"Of course. Just kidding, sir," smiled Bart.

"Of course," returned Wellington II.

Wellington II passed a filled glass of brandy to

Stanley, opened a humidor and passed out his favored imported cigars. He then moved with his own brandy to a surround of large comfortable leather chairs near the center of the room where the two young men joined him, all sitting on cue. Lighting and sampling their cigars, Bart was forced to hold back a cough. He didn't agree with cigars and wondered just why the hell he accepted it in the first place. Turning his head to hide his displeasure he noticed across the room a well stoked fire in a broad overly ornate marble fireplace faced by two large overstuffed high-back chairs. The only other furnishings in the goodly sized library were tables supporting glass encased ships and memorabilia in the form of ship's bells and various ship's fittings taken from favored vessels of days past. Also a few tables with lamps and ash trays to accompany the chairs. And of course there was the bar. Who could read all these books without the aid of a good bottled stimulant, thought Bart.

"So Bartholomew, how goes it amidst the ivy covered halls of my old university?"

Bart was in mid gulp of his brandy, trying to kill the lingering taste of the cigar.

"Oh fine, sir. Wonderful in fact. Especially the ivy covered halls with your name on them," Bart smiled.

Wellington II smiled in return. The comment didn't go unnoticed and was even appreciated. Bart squirmed a bit, not sure if his host appreciated his odd sense of humor.

"And Stanley? Performing well as usual, I expect."

"Of course, sir," answered Stanley.

"Of course," echoed Wellington II.

They sat and sipped their brandy, Wellington II in his grandeur, the boys in bored expectation, until the elder Wellington broke the uncomfortable silence with an attempt at some obligatory social small talk.

"So, young Haile, I understand you, like Stanley, are also a student of law."

"Yes sir," affirmed Bart. "Much more preferable than taking up proctology."

"Um, yes. Of course," responded Wellington II. "I expect your parents are very proud of you. Certainly should be."

"Not really, sir. They're dead."

"Oh, um. Well... Um... I'm so sorry to hear that. Tragic. Tragic indeed."

"Oh, not at all, sir. They died happy," clarified Bart. "Screwing in a railroad Pullman car when the train went off a bridge."

Bart had a way of coming to the point of a conversation and this occasion was no exception causing Stanley to nearly choke on his brandy and Wellington II to search for recovery in his own glass.

"Oh dear, I mean... Yes, well... Fortunate then. Leaving you an estate, I mean. Getting you through university."

"Oh no sir. Haven't got a damn cent.

"But..."

"Full scholarship, sir. I'm a bloody genius."

Stanley started sinking into his chair, fighting laughter while avoiding participation in the conversation. It was this total lack of inhibition that he appreciated most in his good friend Bart which somehow managed to compensated for his own social reserve. This and the fact that Bart's humor tended to draw fun loving ladies like bees to honey. He observed with delight and it seemed Bart was doing fine on his own but he could avoid it only so long and felt obligated to rescue his father whom it seemed was out of his element.

"Well father. How is business these days?" he asked. "Difficult I imagine, with the depression and all?"

Wellington II welcomed the subject change and leaned back, obviously more comfortable in the realm of business than personal chit chat.

"Ah yes, business. Proper you should ask, Stanley. Business. The future. Your future. Things we need to speak about."

"Father, is it necessary to have this conversation again. I've told you many times, I want to build my own life and explore my options independently."

"So, once again you show contempt for the family, the estate and our social standing. Wellington Shipping and Transportation is a large serious concern. All these things came hard and it's your responsibility to…"

Stanley stood, his immediate instinct being to leave the room but he instead searched for a diversionary argument.

"Father, I may as well tell you… I've… Well… Bart

and I…"

Bart perked up. He hadn't a single damn clue where Stanley was going with this and wasn't quite sure if he wanted to tag along, even if this was Stanley's idea of fending off the beast.

"We've done some research and have… um, decided to venture into… um, mining."

Bart silently mouthed the word *mining*, drew on his cigar and choked.

"Mining? Are you insane?" returned Wellington II, looking to Bart for confirmation.

Bart offered only a bewildered yet somehow affirming smile.

"Um, diamonds, actually," continued Stanley. "We've discovered what we think is a healthy deposit of diamonds. Um, in the Indian Ocean."

"That's preposterous! What kind of irresponsible talk is this?" questioned Wellington II, rising to refill his brandy and continuing. "Diamonds? In the Indian Ocean? A pipe dream. A harebrained pipe dream. I won't hear of it and I won't tolerate it and I won't even discuss it."

Then, mysteriously, from across the room came an authoritative voice of reason.

"Oh hell, Junior. Cut the bullshit."

Bart and Stanley turned and looked across the room. From behind one of the large chairs near the fireplace rose grandfather Wellington. He stood tall, domineering, wearing a favorite old smoking jacket, a favorite old touring cap, and holding a large serious glass of Scotch whisky. He drank it down then walked confidently across the room to the bar next to Wellington II and poured another. As he did so he addressed Bart with a bit of advice.

"Better douse that donkey dick your smoking there, Bartholomew. You're starting to turn green."

Bart looked to the cigar and gladly obliged by snuffing it out in a nearby ashtray. Wellington II drew on his brandy and returned to his seat. Grandfather Wellington turned, saluted with his glass, took a manly gulp of the scotch then addressed and pointed with the glass to his son, Wellington II.

"Junior, I've been listening to this silly-ass dribble of yours for years and to your credit I'll give you your due. You certainly do know business and you've tripled the family fortune. Not to mention weathering the stock market crash of twenty-nine and overcoming this damn depression but as God is my witness son you don't know shit from Shinola about kids." Another draw on his scotch and he continued, "Our boy Stanley here is not you and he's not me but he is a Wellington, damned or be gone, and he's his own man and he's got an itch you can't scratch. So why the hell don't you just loosen your self-righteous corset, quit pussy footing around, give the boy your blessing and leave it at that?"

Wellington II sat back in his chair, flustered. Bart hid a smile of approval with a gulp of brandy.

Grandfather Wellington continued. "Son, I know you

think I'm a little ruff around the edges. It's because my father sent me to sea when I was young and I'm a better man for it. Might not impress the neighbors but then who the hell gives a damn. The question is, do you want a boy with character or some damn candy ass who struts around counting money all day? Oh hell, son. He's not going to bring down the empire. He simply wants to get laid and come by his own means on his own terms. I don't know about you but I think that kind of independent attitude is rather admirable, commendable to say the least and though you may believe otherwise, I can remember having such desires, those kinds of days and those feelings."

The senior Wellington moved across the room to the ships under glass and pointed to a model of a three-masted barkentine. He placed his hand on the glass with affection as he continued, "I know it may seem foreign to you but it's not an unproven concept, even for the Wellingtons. Your great grandfather for example, cabin boy to ship's Captain, created the foundation of the Wellington fortune. It didn't come by placating a circle of spongy socialites like that squirrelly bunch out there in the ballroom, you know. It took courage and an appetite for adventure. It took some balls."

Wellington II rose, irritated but properly respectful of his father and knowing there was no way he would emerge victorious in an argument this close to the old man's heart.

"Yes. Well, I suppose I'd better see to our guest," he

said as he rose from his chair.

"Of course, son. You do that," agreed the old man, slapping him on the back. "The decent thing to do."

Wellington II offered all present a nod as he departed the room, "Boys. Merry Christmas."

"Merry Christmas, father," answered Stanley.

"Merry Christmas, Mr. Wellington," said Bart as he stood, "And thank you, sir."

With the departure of Wellington II from the library, grandfather Wellington turned with a smile, snatched up the bottle of scotch and joined Bart and Stanley. As they all sat the old man handed the bottle to Bart then snatched Stanley's lit cigar and popped it in his mouth.

"Now gentlemen," said grandfather Wellington. "What's all this goddamn malarkey about diamonds?"

chapter 4

The rain earlier in the day soaked and rested on the Princeton field just waiting to be churned into a slosh of ugly muck, a deep muddy muck interspersed with a tint of the remaining green grass of the season. Churned up as it had been for the past few hours by the spiked footwear of a group of tired sweaty collegiate gladiators who were now gathered head to head in a circle, interlocked and rocking to and fro to finally explode from the scrummage into a violent tumultuous effort to gain possession and control of that oversized leather egg they called a ball. As they did, the grunts of effort and physical stress mixed with the groans of fleeting physical pain and brutal contact. They fought and scrapped, shins and feet, shoulders and elbows, teeth and gritty turf, all collided and mixed in a vicious symphony of chaos called rugby, a game of endurance and incredible determination. It was also a game loved by our two intrepid ivy leaguers, Stanley and Bart, who were there in the middle of it all running with the best of them. Trying to identify who was who however was a mere guess at best for they were all so encrusted in the brown stew of the wet ball field that their only discernable individual feature seemed to be the color of their eyes. Yet through the fatigue and strain of the game those same eyes flashed bright with excitement and challenge.

"How does it feel to have your stuck-up ass rolling in the mud with the rest of us commoners?" huffed Bart as he ran past Stanley.

"How else can I achieve the level of my idol and…"

He was suddenly interrupted when he was blind sided, blocked and sent rolling to the ground. Bart came to his aid, extended a muddy hand and helped him up.

"Idol. What idol?"

"Bart Haile of course," laughed Stanley, wiping mud from his face. "You know, that guy who laughs in the face of danger, would crawl through hell to reach the stars, leaves the ladies swooning in his absence."

"Damn. Sounds like quite a guy. Like to meet him some time," laughed Bart.

"The opportunity may very well come, my man," smiled Stanley.

"Also sounds like your brain is overheating again."

"We'll only be young once, my man. If it's to be

done it's to be done now."

"Oh no. Don't start that again," said Bart as he turned away, wiping the mud from his hands. "I'm comfortable right where I am. Right here in the mud with the sane people."

The sudden shrill of a whistle froze each player in his muddy tracks and another halted the match altogether, allowing the exhausted players to finally drag themselves off the field. The group of young men caught their breath at the sideline as they gathered their gear then wearily headed for the locker room, moving in a manner reminiscent of a troop of wrung out World War I doughboys coming off a month in the trenches. Bart and Stanley were accompanied by an exceptionally large muscular young man known as Big Tiny Braxton who sucked on a slightly bent and muddied cigar and seemed to tower over another shorter student player by the name of Geoffrey Chrisfield, a geology major. Big Tiny and Chrisfield listened as Bart and Stanley engaged in a conversation that had begun earlier that day and continued through most of the weekly rugby club match.

"You can't be serious, Stanley. He was just some old sailor spouting a bullshit story," insisted Bart. "That's what old sailors do when they can't sail any more. They sit around and get drunk and embellish little old stories until they're great big new lies."

"I don't think so."

"You don't think so. What do you mean you don't think so? You thought that old codger was a loose duck

45

from the minute you saw him but now you don't think so?"

"Well, I've reconsidered."

"No, you're trying to fend off that family beast of yours," insisted Bart as he began exploring a foreign object lodged somewhere in his shorts. "But it's going to come around and bite you in the ass if you don't wise up."

"Now there you go again, Bart. Overreacting," said Stanley. "Just like you did when I had that affair with that Turkish belly dancer."

"I thought I had the affair with the Turkish belly dancer," asked a confused Bart.

"You did. That's why you overreacted when I did."

Big Tiny looked to Chrisfield, "This is starting to get good. I didn't know about the Turkish belly dancer."

"You didn't? I thought everybody knew about that Turkish belly dancer," replied Chrisfield.

"How the hell did you know about the Turkish belly dancer," asked Bart, turning to Chrisfield.

Chrisfield offered only a smile in response.

"Bart, where's your lawyers logic?" asked Stanley. "If the information validates the potential outcome then it's essential that we pursue the course."

"What...what information? What course?" demanded Bart. "And what the hell does that mean anyway?"

Chrisfield tried to offer an explanation, "It means that..."

"I know what it means," insisted Bart, interrupting

Chrisfield. "It means, I still don't know how the hell you found out about that Turkish belly dancer."

"There, you see?" offered Stanley. "The Turkish belly dancer. The perfect example."

"Of what?" asked a frustrated Bart.

"It's about adventure and exploration and opportunity. It's about choosing between a sexy Turkish belly dancer and just another day at the office."

"Yeah," agreed Bart. "But you don't have to go all the way around the world for that kind of adventure."

"Sorry Bart, but you have a vested interest in this venture and I won't let you refrain from your obligations," insisted Stanley.

"Vested? I'm not vested, I'm sensible and you're obsessed. You've been obsessed with this idea ever since last Christmas. Get a damn grip on yourself, will ya."

"I took the map to the archeology department and Professor Huckstep over there said it was authentic."

"So what. That only means it's old. Doesn't mean it's real. My grandmother's old but that doesn't mean she's the Queen of England."

"Is the queen of England old," Big Tiny asked Chrisfield.

"Don't know," shrugged Chrisfield. "Never met her."

Bart reached down to finally discover and carefully removed the irritating chunk of muddy sod from inside his shorts. Looking at the clump of sod he observed, "This is what I subject myself to, balls in the mud and brains in the clouds. You see, playing this game is just as

47

ridiculous as pursuing a sailor's yarn. Why do we do this? Why do *I* do this? And why the hell would you want to chase an old sailor's fable anyway?"

"Because the game is good for the soul," answered Stanley. "And so is the pursuit of fortune and glory. Besides you love rugby. You said it yourself, something about releasing all your inhibitions, although I can't imagine you having any."

"It's a bunch of boys chasing a ball around in the mud. How's that good for the soul?"

Chrisfield looked up at the towering Big Tiny Braxton, "Boys? What boys?"

"It's an uncharted island, remember?" continued Bart. "It doesn't even have a name. You can't prove it's there if it's not there... not charted. I mean... Well, you know what I mean."

"Exactly. If it were charted then everybody would know about it and there wouldn't be any diamonds would there? Not only that, I had the old sailor's ship, the Saint Jane, researched. Her disappearance is a matter of record just like the old guy said. And why are you objecting so much anyway? The map's half yours. You'll be a full partner."

"Yeah, like that old sailor. He was a partner and all he came away with was a sliced up face and a bum leg. And his life, barely," replied Bart. "Um, if you can believe him, that is."

Chrisfield, listening with intense interest, tried to offer an observation but couldn't get a word in over

Bart's continued animated protests.

"Actually, I think…"

"Crazy," Bart interrupted Chrisfield. "Just plain crazy. Maybe not for you but crazy for me. You can afford to gamble, you've got nothing to lose but I could lose everything."

"Bart, you don't have anything," observed Stanley.

"Yeah, that's true. But I'm on my way to having more of it."

Stanley and Big Tiny looked to Bart, puzzled.

Chrisfield tried again, "You know, it's not so…"

"And what about your father?" Bart interrupted Chrisfield again. He's not exactly fond of the idea. He could cut you off. Disinherit you. Then what will you do?"

A knowing sly smile crawled over Stanley's dirty mud caked face that was quickly detected by Bart.

"What?" asked an aggravated Bart. "What? I've seen that look before. When you absconded with that Turkish belly dancer."

"You have to tell me about that Turkish belly dancer," Big Tiny said to Chrisfield.

"Don't you tell him anything," ordered Bart.

"Well, she had this mustache," Chrisfield told Big Tiny. "And a really big…"

"Imagination," interrupted Bart.

Stanley continued his smile in silence as they walked on to the locker room where they found the rest of the muddy Princeton rugby doughboys shedding their filthy uniforms and entering the showers. The four young men did the same and as the water transformed them from sweaty mud people to a more recognizable species, Bart continued to argue his case.

"It's just insane that's all," Bart's voice echoed off the tiled shower walls. "We'd need a ship and a crew and if that old sailor's telling the truth… a howitzer canon… a small army. Hell, maybe a large army. Not that that old guy included a lot of details. And then maybe…"

Chrisfield finally broke in, determined to offer his opinion, "You know Wellington, it's not really that far fetched, quite reasonable in fact. Diamonds are usually found at the site of formerly active volcanoes. Pushed up from far below the earth's surface millions of years ago. As we all know the Pacific Ocean and especially that part of the world is just littered with volcanic islands."

"There you go, Bart," Stanley offered in defense. "Chrisfield here is a geology major. He doesn't think it's so crazy."

"Yeah well, I'm a law major but that doesn't mean I can kick Al Capone's ass," replied Bart as he dug some mud from his ear. "Volcanoes? I didn't know that. Oh that's even better. Phony maps, mysterious beast, volcanoes. Yeah, we'll certainly need an army all right. An army of psychiatrists."

"An army," echoed Stanley who went on to shower in silent thought until an idea evolved and the smile returned. Then when he exited the shower Stanley went to the center of the locker room, stood atop a bench and turned to face the rest of the members of the rugby club.

"Gentlemen, may I have your attention!"

The young men, some still muddy and some clean, all gathered around. Bart moved to his locker, curious and wary of the look on Stanley's face.

"Gentlemen, I'd like to tell you all a story about an old sailor and a map," began Stanley.

Bart, dejected, plopped down on a bench and plunged his wet face into a towel.

There was no fog on this evening nor was there any moon to speak of, resulting in the large sign which hung near the entrance of the dock to be barely readable. The headlights of an approaching vehicle however, momentarily brought the sign to life just long enough to make out the faded lettering that boldly proclaimed WELLINGTON SHIPPING LINES. The shiny black Duesenberg limousine glided prominently past the sign, through the gate and along the dock, its top uncharacteristically stacked safari like with assorted gear and baggage. Eventually the limousine eased to a full stop near the foot of a gangplank where its chauffeur exited the car and quickly opened the rear door. From inside emerged Stanley and Bart looking up to discover a classic three-masted ship. It was the Crimson Glory, a big, beamy, proud, well-seasoned cargo ship and yes, one of those prized vessels immortalized under glass in the Wellington library.

Above, Captain Horatio Buckmaster, a man in his

mid 40s, experienced and confident, came to the side of the ship and peered down at the arriving limousine. He then called to some nearby crewmen, "You men there. Go ashore and bring up that gear."

"Aye Skipper," replied the crewmen as they quickly obeyed and made way down the gangplank to assist the new arrivals. As they began dislodging and unloading the baggage and gear another passenger emerged from the vehicle, grandfather Wellington. As usual, he wore an aged but comfortable English wool sporting coat, a silk scarf, and his favorite tweed touring cap. Essentially he was no different than on the night of the Christmas gala and as usual, not caring whom he did or did not impress by his appearance. After exiting the vehicle he looked up to the ship and grew an affectionate smile.

Upon seeing the elder Wellington, Captain Buckmaster offered up a respectful salute of recognition that Wellington acknowledged with a casual salute of his own.

Stanley, with a sea bag slung over his shoulder, came to his grandfather's side.

"Grandfather, I…"

The old man looked on him with pride and approval. "No need for words, son," he politely interrupted. "I only wish I were going with you."

They shook hands until the formal handshake grew into a manly embrace. Stanley then turned away and finding a space between the crewmen hauling the gear up the gangplank, began to ascend when he was accidentally bumped by another crewman on his way down.

"Oh, sorry, me boyo."

It was the Wellington's Christmas Gala Irish poet doorman who after bumping into and apologizing to Stanley glanced over to grandfather Wellington and offered up a restrained confidential salute of his own. The senior Wellington nodded recognition then turned to Bart who was loaded down with baggage as he started for the ship.

"Mr. Haile," Called Wellington.

Bart stopped and turned. Perceiving and understanding the look on Wellington's face he offered without hesitation, "I will, sir. Like he was my own brother."

The old man nodded appreciation and Bart turned away to board the ship.

As he ascended the gangplank he continued mumbling to himself, "A brother? What kind of a brother would do this to me? Crazy son of a…"

Bart looked up to fully appreciate the ship for the first time, growing more apprehensive as he viewed its daunting complex characteristics.

"Oh boy, it's a boat. It's a real boat. I don't know shit about boats. And on the ocean, that's great too. I'm going to puke. I'm going to puke all the way to… wherever the hell… Uncharted… Perdition. That's what that crazy old salt called it, perdition."

With Stanley and Bart safely aboard the elder Wellington gave the ship a final look of approval then turned and entered his limousine.

Moments later the vehicle cruised slowly near one of the Wellington warehouses coming to a halt near the building's shadowy entrance. Grandfather Wellington sat patiently while the door of the Duesenberg opened. Out of the shadows limped the old sailor who paused, acknowledged Wellington with a friendly nod and slid easily onto the seat next to him. The chauffeur closed the door then drove the two men off into the night.

chapter 5

Bart was making his way through a below decks passage of the Crimson Glory, lost, overloaded and struggling with baggage as he searched for his berth. Lifting a bag that blocked his vision in order to enter through a door he suddenly heard a warning in the form of a deep strong voice.

"Heads up there sailor!"

When he peaked around the burdensome load he surprisingly spied a flying object souring straight for his head. Desperate, he dropped everything just in time to catch - a rugby ball. He looked at the ball then to its launching source, unexpectedly finding thirteen members of the Princeton University Rugby Club sprawled about the ship's mess, sipping coffee and laughing.

Bart, thinking only he and Stanley were making the journey, was almost speechless. Almost. "Well, I'll be a..."

"...a monkey's uncle?" laughed Chrisfield.

"Well no. More like a real man at a little girls tea party," corrected Bart.

Objects of disagreement flew through the air from all around the mess at Bart who dropped the ball and tripped and fell over the baggage when he tried to dodge the borage. The rugby boys roared with laughter.

"It's nice to know there's more than one fool on this boat," laughed Bart as he lay sprawled atop the baggage.

The rugby boy's roar of laughter carried from the ship's mess to above decks and topside where Captain Buckmaster and Stanley stood looking out over New York harbor. With the passing of the evening the harbor had gone to rest and the noisy clamor of the sea trade had yielded to the gentle lapping of water and distant echoes from the city.

The Captain, teasing a little smoke out of a hand carved ivory pipe observed, "That's an interesting crew you've got there, young Wellington."

Stanley smiled and nodded agreement.

"They have any sailing experience?" inquired the Captain.

"Most do. But that's not the reason they're here," replied Stanley.

"I trust I'll be informed of the purpose of this voyage."

"Of course, sir. As soon as we've cleared the Outer Banks."

"Not before?"

Stanley offered no response and the Captain pried no further, taking the young man at his word. Stanley turned and looked about the ship, sizing her up and becoming much impressed.

"Say, I thought my father discarded all these sailing vessels years ago in favor of steamers. Sold or traded them all off."

"He did."

"I don't understand. She still carries the Wellington flag."

"She's your grandfather's favorite. He saved her. Purchased her aside from the company... on the sly you might say," said the Captain with a confidential smile.

"Of course. Sounds like something he'd do."

"I'm surprised you didn't know."

"No reason to I suppose," said Stanley.

"But Mr. Wellington. The Crimson Glory is *your* ship. *Your* registry," clarified the Captain.

"What... What are you saying?"

"You own this ship, sir. And everything about her. I've been in your employ for, oh nearly nine years now. And if you don't mind my bragging a bit, she's been fairly profitable in spite of her years. There's no expense to the wind, as your grandfather is fond of saying."

Stanley was set aback as he looked to the Captain then again over the ship with newly appreciative eyes.

"Something tells me this is going to be a very interesting voyage. Interesting indeed," laughed Captain Buckmaster as he slapped Stanley on the back. "Well then, I'm going to retire and leave you alone to get acquainted with the old lady. She's well kept and well treated and you'll find she's old but she's forgiving and dependable. Your grandfather would tell you that as well. He cut his teeth on this ship many years ago."

With that, Captain Buckmaster left Stanley alone on deck as he made for the hatch and below to retire for the night. As he did he turned and offered up one last comment.

"We sail with the morning tide, Mr. Wellington. I'd suggest you call your men to order then all of you get some rest. By what little I *do* know I suspect it's going to be a long voyage."

Following Captain Buckmaster's departure, Stanley turned, spread his hands on the ship's rail and looked out over the harbor. He breathed deeply, closed his eyes then opened them to the New York City skyline where there rose above all else the Empire State Building. And to think, he mused and smiled, this all began with Bart wanting to see a silly monkey movie.

A loud CLANG rang out when a large cast iron frying pan slammed against the bulkhead of the galley. Big Tiny Braxton's eyes grew wide with fear as he ducked to avoid what would have been certain death in the form of that same lethal weapon when it passed nearby again, colliding with the passageway door and barely missing Bart who had just arrived and was about to enter.

"Oh shit!" exclaimed Bart. "What the..."

"I was just looking for a snack," explained Big Tiny.

The iron pan rose again, gripped firmly by the hands of a five foot nothing short wild-eyed crazed Chinese cook who babbled threats continuously in his native tongue. Bart entered the galley carefully, crossing and bumping into Big Tiny who was desperately backing away in the opposite direction and struck his head on the low entrance. Bart stepped in and threw up his hands as though he had just been cornered in some cheesy Western movie.

"No no! Wait! Stop!" he pleaded of the Chinaman.

The little Chinese cook stood his ground, continuing to express what must have been the Oriental equivalent of the entire unabridged international sailor's profane four letter lexicon. In a quest for peace, waving his hands, Bart attempted to bridge the language barrier, which he had somehow quickly deduced was the crux of the problem at hand.

"No no. You... You stoppee. You no can chop chop big man with big iron pan. You makee big man get dead. Captainson no likee big man get dead."

The cook grew silent but continued to hold the pan at the ready. Bart smiled, believing he was making progress.

"Big man same same likee fuzzy little panda bear,"

said Bart, patting Big Tiny's belly to demonstrate his meaning and show Big Tiny's harmlessness. "He no hurt little China man. Little China man put down big pan now, okay. No more chop chop. No more whack whack. No good you hurt little fuzzy panda big man. You savvy?"

The cook lowered the pan and stared at Bart for a long puzzled moment, then said finally, "I don't know where the hell you learned your Chinese, pal, but I wouldn't advise you use it in an Oriental restaurant. You're likely to end up with a bowl full of pig shit and chicken lips."

Bart stared. Big Tiny stared. The cook tossed the deadly pan on the table with a bang, wiped his hands on his apron and extended one in greeting to Bart who continued to stare but eventually accepted with caution.

"My name is Soo," said the Chinese cook.

"Sue?" returned Bart, quickly releasing the cook's hand and looking to Big Tiny.

Big Tiny shrugged his shoulders and subtly shook a limp wrist, his silent gesture of explanation regarding the cook's feminine name.

"No no, damnit. Not Sue. Soo," clarified the cook.

Bart stared. Big Tiny stared.

"Soo Lee Min Jones. Everybody calls me Jonesy," said the cook. "I'm the cook on this ship and I'll kill anybody who farts around in my galley. Got that?"

Bart and Big Tiny both nod understanding.

"Good. Now get the hell out of here," Jonesy

instructed Bart. "I have work to do."

He then retrieved a large cleaver and turned his attention to a pile of vegetables on a nearby chopping block. The first victim was a head of cabbage as the cleaver came down with lightning speed and resounding force. The cabbage offered little resistance, falling over in two equal pieces. Jonesy turned to Big Tiny and smiled. Big Tiny swallowed nervously as he unconsciously ran his hand across his neck.

"And take that big fuzzy panda bear with you," added Jonesy.

Bart stared. Big Tiny stared. Then suddenly the culture lesson ended when it was interrupted by the entrance of a much excited Geoffrey Chrisfield.

"Hey fellahs. Topside. It's Lady Liberty," announced Chrisfield.

Bart, Big Tiny and Chrisfield arrived topside just as the Crimson Glory was sailing past the Statue of Liberty.

"Say, Bart. What's all this stuff about a curse and a monster?" asked Big Tiny.

Bart squinted as he came into the morning light and looked up to Lady Liberty towering far above their ship's mast and billowing sails. The prominent lady, standing there so very tall on her island seemed to offer Bart some kind of premonition of which he failed to grasp.

"Monster?" answered Bart, looking up to the giant lady. "Oh, it's no big deal."

chapter 6

Weeks later the Crimson Glory was cutting through the Pacific like the proudest of eagles, soaring beneath a bright blue sky with a full spread of canvas and bloated sails. Some crew were busying themselves dangerously in the rigging, others laboring on deck assisted by adventuresome members of the Princeton Rugby Club. By now the crew and the Princeton boys had bonded into one company, becoming a sailing team Captain Buckmaster occasionally referred to as the Bungling Back East Gang. Noting that both his crew and all of the Wellington party were Easterners but for himself, a product of Oregon, and Jonesy who originated in California.

Even Bart had overcome his initial spell of

nauseating seasickness and constant stomach-churning regurgitation to master the basic chores of seamanship, his favorite of course, ringing the ship's bell. As he expressed to his contemporaries at this days early meal setting in the ship's mess, "I'm beginning to understand the lore and adventure of the sea but damn if I wouldn't care to put down a decent meal topped off with my grandmother's own bread pudding."

He was swiftly whacked on the back of the head with a large wooden spoon, Jonesy's favorite utensil and weapon of choice.

"You have bread pudding for a brain," said an unappreciated Jonesy, leaving all present to make a mental note not to criticize the little man's cooking. At least not while he was around.

"Not so," one of the boys informed Jonesy. Mr. Haile here is considered to be a near genius. The academic pride of Princeton."

"Umf," responded an unimpressed Jonesy. "You'd never know it judging by his language skills."

Following the morning meal in question, Stanley, Bart, Captain Buckmaster, Chrisfield, and a few others remained in the ship's mess. Stanley and the Captain were huddled over the old map, comparing it with the current charts of the day. The map was composed mostly of a rough likeness of the island along with its coordinates in longitude and latitude.

"What do you estimate our arrival time to be then,"

Stanley asked of the Captain.

"I'd say a week. Maybe less. Depending on the winds and how true this map of yours is. But I suggest we put in for supplies before we get there," recommended the Captain. "We've enough to hold us over but since our stay will be indefinite and we're not sure what we'll find or if we'll even find the island..."

"Re-supply. Where do you recommend?" asked Stanley.

"Sumatra maybe or better yet here, New Guinea," answered the Captain, pointing to a point on the map. "There's a port there that's adequate for our needs and it won't take us far off our course. And they're not the kind of folks to ask questions. After which we can run the islands and round Sumatra then it's all pretty much strait sailing."

Stanley looked over his shoulder to Bart who caught both his glance and meaning. Both recalled the old sailor's tale about New Guinea and Borneo.

"Why not Borneo? I hear they have a real spiffy jail," offered Bart sarcastically.

"Not practical," answered the Captain, Bart's comment evading him.

"Right," agreed Bart.

"Now, this island of yours," continued Captain Buckmaster. "There's no guarantee it even exists. Though I've heard a few bar room tales over the years. About a cursed island with some kind of monster. Hear the legend even turned into some silly Hollywood picture show. Always wrote it off as sailor's bilge myself. Until I read your map that is. I've seen a few of these old Portuguese maps over the years and I'd say this one's legitimate."

"Oh, then you read Portuguese?" asked Stanley.

"No, not hardly. I had Jonesy read it."

"Jonesy. The cook?"

"Sure," said the Captain as a matter of fact. "Jonesy's a Rhodes Scholar. Um, Oxford, twenty-seven I believe. Speaks more languages than a Libyan trader."

Everyone in the room caught the Captain's words and grew silent in disbelief.

"Now, about your cargo. I think it's time your boys were introduced and familiarized with it," suggested the Captain. "In case they may need some of it. Can't be too careful in this part of the world you know."

"Agreed," said Stanley. "But after New Guinea. No sense in asking for trouble."

"Very well."

"What do you make our time to port then?" asked Stanley.

"Better part of a day or two, or into a third. Then a day to take on supplies."

Just then Jonesy entered the mess with a pot of fresh coffee. They all turned and stared at him with new found respect. Jonesy paused and stared back.

"What?" he asked. "What's wrong? You don't like my coffee?"

They continued to stare in surprised silent

65

astonishment of their newly revealed resident Rhodes Scholar. Jonesy set the coffee down then turned and mumbled in Chinese something about crazy ass white men as he exited the room.

"A Rhodes Scholar?" said Bart.

"Crazy ass white men," repeated Jonesy.

It was a bustling little frontier kind of port, New Guinea style. Wild in its own way but inviting if you were capable of self-preservation. Moored along the docks were ships of various kinds and sizes including the Crimson Glory and a rusty ill kept Greek tramp steamer nearby named the Ictinus.

Captain Buckmaster laid a careful eye on both his ship and the dock as he roamed the Crimson Glory's deck. He was also closely observing the supplies being brought aboard by his crew.

"Make haste there men? We sail the tide in two hours," he said as he checked his pocket watch. He looked down on the dock where he spied the crewman they had all come to know simply as, Irish.

"You there, Irish."

Irish paused, a wooden crate on his shoulders, and looked up to the Captain.

"Aye Skipper?"

"You best go and gather up Wellington's boys. Two hours mind you. We sail in two hours time."

"Aye Skipper," Irish acknowledged as he passed the crate to another crewman and set off up the dock and into the nearby town.

The port town was buzzing with a mix of nationalities hocking their wares or buying others. Islanders, Europeans, Eastern, Middle Eastern, Oriental, even some native head hunter cannibals had come out of the frontier woodwork for some limited urbanizing. Through all of this ethnic mix wandered Irish in search of Wellington's wayward rugby boys. During his wandering he eventually came to pass a produce stand at which he saw little Jonesy picking through a pile of strange and peculiar food and adding it to his basket, all the while arguing in some unfamiliar foreign language with the food stand's highly animated vendor.

"Yeah, yeah. So's your mother," declared Jonesy in English as he flipped the vendor a coin and walked away.

Irish laughed at Jonesy's lack of diplomacy then paused in the middle of the crowded street and listened tentatively. Ah hah, he thought as he turned to discover a nearby bar around a corner from which came the sound of young men chanting a college fight song.

"In Princeton town we've got a team that knows the way to play.

With Princeton spirit back of them, they're sure to win the day.

With cheers and song we'll rally 'round the cannon as of yore.

And Nassau's walls will echo with the Princeton Tiger's roar."

"Not quite up to Irish standards," Irish said to himself. "But a tune is a tune and that sounds like our boys."

He followed the noise as well as his nose to the drinking establishment, paused at the threshold confirming the chanting was in English and was indeed his lost boys, then entered to discover a spacious, if not cavernous, old place in which there had probably been served a million shots to a million sailors on a million nights with a whore house above and a shanghai business on the side. A place where legends were made and lies had been told, a true place of true ill repute. In the center of what passed as a dance floor Irish found the rugby boys, all fourteen of them, bent over in an interlocking intoxicated unsteady rugby scrummage chanting their fight song and looking more foolish than any of the million who had ever come before.

Irish checked the old clock on the wall, determining he had just enough time to quench that nagging bit of dryness in back of his throat. He then sauntered over to the long bar and ordered a whisky. Receiving his drink, he turned, raised the glass to his American comrades and saluted them with a bit of his impromptu homegrown poetry.

"There once was a girl in New Guinea, who unlike Gaelic mums was quite skinny. But once on me lap…"

Irish paused briefly when he spied at the door and entering the bar the ill kept crew of the ill kept Greek tramp steamer, all appearing to be ill tempered, ugly and thirsty. He continued his prose with caution.

"But once on me lap, a bit of this led to that, and she soon became…"

The Greeks wondered in, took a gander at the circle of upturned Ivy League asses and began to chuckle, spelling imminent trouble and causing Irish to discontinue his doggerel.

"What's this?" observed a bristle faced burly Greek sailor, in Greek of course.

"I think maybe a bunch of clucking hens," answered another.

The Greeks all laughed and began clucking like chickens. The burly one walked over to one of the upturned asses, inspected it humorously, then placed a hand on each cheek.

"The last time I saw a clucking hen like this I made her sing like a rooster," he laughed, looking at his fellow shipmates and patting the upturned ass as he would that of a sumptuous woman.

The Greek sailors roared with laughter. When the burly one turned back, the ass in question rose and turned and he found himself facing a very large and unimpressed Big Tiny Braxton who held a rugby ball in one hand and a bottle of beer in the other.

Irish forgot his poetry, quickly downed his whisky and drew a cross on his chest.

"May the saints have mercy on our souls and our sins upcoming never be told," he prayed to himself.

Big Tiny offered the Greek a smile, who smiled in return and upon seeing the rugby ball, took it and held it up for all to see.

"Oh look! Our hen has laid an egg," he declared.

The crew of the Ictinus exploded with insulting laughter and the affronting burly Greek turned back to face Big Tiny who continued to smile, seemingly enjoying the joke. Big Tiny then politely took back the ball, handed the bottle of beer to the Greek, spun the ball on the index finger of his left hand and while the Greek focused on the spinning ball, Big Tiny nailed him with a powerful right cross, sending him across the room and into the rest of the Ictinus crew.

The commotion brought the rest of the rugby boys to their senses, causing them to break apart and rise to investigate. In doing so they exposed a near naked girl standing bewildered in the center of their circle. Angered and quick tempered, the Greeks retaliated and, as they say, all hell broke loose, bringing everyone to beat on everyone except for a very inebriated Bart Haile who remained holding his position in the circle until he finally realized he was alone. When he rose, a flying Greek sailed over his head and crashed against the wall. The girl screamed and scurried off leaving a bewildered Bart to turn and squint at the battered man lying in a heap at his feet.

"Do I know you?" slurred a drunken Bart.

The Greek could only moan in return.

"Hmf, a snob eh," replied Bart. "Must be a damn

Yalie."

It was a colorful and classic bar fight. Chairs flew, bodies flew, tables flew, chairs broke, bodies broke, tables broke, Big Tiny knocked heads, a wily Chrisfield threw traditional boxing jabs and then of course there was Irish on top of the bar, a bottle in each hand, dancing a jig so enthusiastically one could almost hear the bagpipes. Irish danced from one end of the bar to the other all the while crowning one Greek after another with a bottle but not, of course, without first sampling the bottle's contents.

Then suddenly, from out of nowhere came a loud penetrating two-fingered whistle and an announcement stating clearly and fluently in Greek -

"ATTENTION CREW OF THE ICTINUS. YOUR SHIP IS ON FIRE!"

The fighting Greeks froze.

"Fire? Fire? FIRE!" they shouted in a panic as they snatched up their near dead and bleeding wounded and hurried from the bar to go to the aid of their vessel.

The rugby boys of the Crimson Glory, the Princeton segment of the Bungling Back East Gang, stood huffing, puffing and battered but not defeated. All eyes turned to discover Jonesy standing by the door with his basket of strange food. Big Tiny wiped his nose clear of blood, looked up and questioned the little Chinese cook.

"What the hell did you say to them?"

"I told them you were escaped Siberian blood sucking leprous ridden psychotics who have sex with animals and Greek sailors," smiled Jonesy.

They all offered Jonesy a tired drunken smile and began nursing their wounds. Bart swaggered up to and leaned on the bar. Behind him plopped down a victorious Irish with a fresh bottle of whisky.

"Yalies," stated Bart in triumphant disdain.

"Absolutely," agreed Irish.

chapter 7

Captain Buckmaster and Stanley were standing on the deck of the Crimson Glory signing off on the recently acquired ship's stores when they heard in the distance the Princeton University fight song or at best a poor rendition. When they looked up they saw the rugby boys parading down the dock in formation, Irish leading the way with a broom for a drum major's baton in one hand and balancing the basket of Jonesy's weird food on his head with the other. He was followed by Big Tiny who was carrying on his shoulders one Soo Lee Min Jones, Oxford Rhodes Scholar and now local hero. Jonesy brandished a royal scepter in the form of a bottle of booze in one hand and cradled the rugby ball in the other. Behind them followed the staggering formation of the rest of the drunken and battered Princeton ivy leaguers.

Nearby on the Ictinus, a bruised black and blue Greek sailor looked out over the ship to also discover the returning Crimson Glory victors. The sailor called to his fellow shipmates who immediately began to gather together, picking up pipes, tools and other potential weapons along the way. They all moved to disembark and confront the parade on the dock below. That is until from above, near the bridge of their ship, an imposing Captain gripped a rail and bellowed with undisputed authority down to his crew.

"If you men leave this ship I swear I will trade your asses to cannibals for a jug of cold wine and a hot woman," threatened their Captain, in Greek of course.

The Greek crewmen all halted; disappointed they couldn't defend their honor. They instead moved grudgingly to line the side of their ship and look down on the passing parade.

When the Crimson Glory parade passed the Ictinus, drum major Irish called his troops to order.

"Right then lads. Here we go now," he ordered.

His little company stood smartly, as much as possible at least.

"Crimson Glory! Eyyyes left!"

They all turned their heads sharply as they marched past, looking up to the Ictinus crew. Jonesy tossed the bottle, contemptuously smashing it against the hull of their ship, agitating the already angry Greeks. Irish continued his direction.

"Presennnnnnt… arms!"

They all stopped and with the exception of Irish who was carrying Jonesy's basket of weird food and Big Tiny who was carrying Jonesy, the entire group turned their backs to the Ictinus, dropped their trousers and mooned the Greeks. Jonesy contributed to the group insult by extending a one-finger salute. This threw the Greeks into a fury of angry protest, beating on the rails of the Ictinus, cursing and offering a few spiteful salutes of their own. Then Irish resumed command.

"Crimson Glory! Attennnnn… tion!"

The drunken rugby boys snatched up their trousers and stood tall.

"Forwarrrrrd… march!"

Off they marched, ordered, proud, victorious, and sloppy as hell. Bringing up the rear stepped Bart, much more inebriated than the rest. He turned back to the Ictinus to offer a final word of insult.

"Yalies!"

And with that final word his trousers slipped down, fully bearing his ass, tripping and lurching him forward to nearly fall on his face. The Greeks burst with laughter all the while continuing to extend insults.

"Might I suggest we set sail immediately following the boarding of your party, Mr. Wellington," said a worried Captain Buckmaster, having witnessed the parade incident.

"Suggest hell," exclaimed Stanley. "Cast off now,

Captain! While we still have a ship to sail on!"

Stanley pointed in the direction of the Ictinus where the Captain looked to also see her riotous angry Greek crew had gone against their own Captain's wishes and decided to pursue the rugby boys. He turned quickly and began barking orders all about the ship.

"All crew stand ready! Lose those lines fore and aft. Prepare to draw up the gangplank as soon as our people come aboard. And prepare to repel boarders if necessary!"

The crew of the Crimson Glory looked up to the Captain unbelieving of his final order. Captain Buckmaster pointed to the dock and the approaching Greeks and repeated his order.

"I said, prepare to repel boarders damnit, and do it smartly!"

The crew all rushed to carry out the Captains orders while Stanley rushed to the side of the ship yelling down to his marching men who were again crooning their school fight song and ignorant of the oncoming herd of angry Greeks behind them.

"BART! IRISH! RUN! RUN!" he yelled, waving his arms to gain their attention.

Bart looked up to Stanley, returned the wave and extended his ever-appealing shit-eating smile.

"Behind you!" warned Stanley emphatically. "Look behind you! Irish! Tiny! Behind you! The Greeks!"

None of the group caught Stanley's desperate pleas, all being absorbed in their slapdash rendition of the

Princeton fight song. Until Jonesy that is. Possibly the soberest of them all and having an ear for language, Jonesy somehow filtered out the song and deciphered Stanley's desperate warning. That plus the fact he could see Stanley desperately jumping up and down and pointing to the approaching Greeks. When he looked back he discovered the threat first hand.

"Holy shit!" exclaimed Jonesy. In Chinese.

"What?" asked Big Tiny.

"Holy shit!" Jonesy repeated, again in Chinese, pointing desperately back to the onrushing Greeks.

Big Tiny looked up with a smile then turned easily to see why Jonesy was so agitated. It took him only a second to realize the approaching peril, even under the influence of nearly a dozen beers. The enraged Greeks were at a full trot now, each carrying some manner of dangerous implement, intent on drawing blood.

"GREEKS!" yelled Big Tiny, his heavy voice having no problem penetrating and overcoming the babbling school fight song. They all got the message and scrambled for the safety of the Crimson Glory. Big Tiny quickly dumped Jonesy who, still carrying the rugby ball, sprinted through the now drunken scurrying group and along the crowded dock for safety, all the while looking like, though on a much smaller scale, none other than the great Red Grange.

Obviously the rugby boys' present condition limited their speed although the situation was quickly sobering. The Greeks, having the element of surprise were quickly closing the gap, so much so they were right on their heals as they reached and sprinted up the Crimson Glory's gangplank. Nearly overrun and captured by three of the fastest Greeks, the last of the pursued, Irish and Bart, dove from the gangplank to the deck of the ship just as the gangplank fell away into the water. The Crimson Glory drifted away from her mooring with her crew, as per the Captains orders, standing ready at the rails with all available implements to repel boarders but none came for none of the Greeks could bridge the growing space between the dock and ship. Everyone breathed relief. Lying on the deck, Irish and Bart burst into laughter, eventually joined by the entire crew until the jovial moment came to an abrupt end by Captain Buckmaster.

"Where's Jonesy?" asked the Captain.

Everyone looked around, shrugged, then looked again with no results. Then a riotous noise rose from back on the dock and when the ship's company looked over they discovered a desperate Jonesy, still carrying the rugby ball, sprinting in and out, to and fro, back and forth, through the pursuing angry Greeks, all the while screaming desperately in what seemed to be five different languages. All meaning the same thing.

"Holy shit! Holy shit! Holy shit!"

"Jonesy!" yelled Bart. "Run man! Run!"

A remedy to Jonesy's situation flashed through Stanley's mind and he quickly looked to the dock then to the ship's rigging. He rushed to the side of the ship, climbed her rigging to the main mast spar, snatched a line then yelled down to Jonesy.

"Jonesy! Here!"

Little Jonesy, still running and dodging the Greeks, glanced up and quickly grasp Stanley's plan though he didn't know, with the ship pulling away from the dock, it would be a one shot opportunity. In addition, failure meant a desperate swim to catch his ship.

The ship's company of the Crimson Glory now lined the side of their vessel and began cheering Jonesy on as though he were the last hope in the final moments of the Rose Bowl Game. This gave the little cook renewed enthusiasm as he came back for a final round through the gauntlet of enraged Greeks. Into the mouth of the dragon he went, courageously clenching the ball for pride of ship, cutting left then right, dodging, sprinting, sliding and *Holy Shitting* in various languages. A final look up to the ship to gain his bearings and then the final sprint for the end zone. At that same instant Stanley grasp the line then threw himself out and away in the opposite direction, knowing when the line came taut it would swing him down in an arc that would just barely reach the bulkhead of the dock. Jonesy had to pass only one more obstacle, one more angry Greek, the burly guy who took the first blow that started it all. As big as the man was he was also fast and agile. Jonesy faked but the Greek didn't bite, faked again but again the Greek won out. Then Jonesy, quick witted and cerebral, took a whole different approach and simply stopped.

"Okay," huffed a tired Jonesy, in Greek. "I give up."

The big burly man rose from his attacking crouch and smiled victoriously then Jonesy launched and landed a penetrating right foot square in the big Greek's gonads. When the unbearable pain quickly doubled the man over, Jonesy took three steps, jumped, launched himself off the Greek's back and into the air where he was met and caught by Stanley then swung back to the safety of the ship. All on the ship went wild with enthusiastic approval while the crew of the Ictinus stood on the dock, dejected. Jonesy was raised above the Crimson Glory company and paraded about as though he had indeed just won the Rose Bowl and to prove it he still possessed and held high with pride Big Tiny's rugby ball. Little Jonesy, to date appreciated for his intellect and unappreciated for his cuisine, was now a certified hero in the eyes of one and all, and for the rest of the voyage would walk a little taller. A *little* taller.

Stanley, meanwhile, melted away to join the Captain where he settled for a simple pat on the back and a beer soaked smile of approval from his good friend Bart.

"Yalies."

chapter 8

Bart and the rest of the rugby boys sat gathered in the cargo hold. It was the *morning after* and however they may have appeared, it certainly wasn't athletic. They were a subdued, seriously beat up and hung over group of young men with heads down, black eyes and sporting a few bandages as trophies of their great battle with the Spartans of the Ictinus. When Stanley and Irish came through the hatch and down the gangway they paused as they saw the state of Princeton's finest, inspiring Irish to sit down easily on the gangway step, smile and offer up a lyric.

"To New Guinea there came a group of young lads full of vinegar, guts and guile. Then came some foul Greeks, a good time for ta seek, who absconded... in disgrace… and denial."

The hung over war torn group slowly raised their heads. From one came a chuckle, then another, and another until they all rose and burst into victorious laughter, forgetting their painful state altogether. Stanley and Irish descended the rest of the gangway joining the boys who began offering Irish compliments and congratulations on his poignant half-ass poetry then began recounting their valorous achievements against the Greeks in the battle of the New Guinea Do Drop In. As they did, Stanley pulled down a stowed crowbar and approached a stack of wooden crates. He jammed the crowbar in the nearest, ripped open the top, then reached in and withdrew a brand new Thompson machine gun.

Upon seeing this the conversation among the group quickly subsided and they all stared at Stanley's marvel of modern technology. He handed the weapon to Chrisfield who accidentally pointed it at Irish's head. Irish calmly and carefully moved it away with a single finger. Ripping open another crate, Stanley brought out an elephant gun and handed it to one of the others. He then brought out a bazooka and of course handed it to Big Tiny. Big Tiny smiled and inspected the weapon with the joy of a young boy who just received his first bicycle.

"We've also got Winchester repeater rifles, forty-fives, dynamite and… oh yeah, a flamethrower," smiled Stanley. "And there's plenty of ammo for all."

Bart stared, surprised, and mouthed to himself, "A

flame thrower?"

"Tools of the trade, gentlemen," continued Stanley. "Courtesy of grandfather Wellington. Just in case."

They all moved in around the crates and began withdrawing and inspecting the weapons.

"Our resident poet, Irish here," continued Stanley. "Formerly of the Irish Republican… Well, lets just say he's talented."

They all laughed and Irish saluted.

"Well, Irish here is going to educate us on the finer points of these… impressive hunting utensils. And I expect, as in all things, you Princeton pirates will be masters before we reach our destination."

As they poured over the crates, laughter and low discussion commenced. Chrisfield, while speaking to Big Tiny, once again allowed the serious end of the Thompson to wonder and point at Irish's head. Irish carefully took possession of the weapon and placed it back in the crate. Suddenly the loud roar of an engine was heard above decks then faded as quickly as it had come causing them to exchange puzzled looks. Then the engine noise returned, this time sounding closer, stronger and then it again faded. Stanley quickly started up the gangway and made his way topside followed by Bart and the others. As the group emerged into the light their attention was quickly drawn to the sky and the thunderous noisy engine of a biplane, a classic old Jennie, diving dead straight for the ship, sure to strike its mass of rigging. The Jennie banked and veered off, missing the ship by an uncomfortably short distance then rose, barrel rolled, and headed again for the Crimson Glory.

All eyes of the ship's company were on the sky as they scrambled about, not knowing what to expect and not sure if they should seek refuge from the erratic aircraft. Now it flew just above the waves coming closer, closer, then quickly climbed to just barely miss the top of the mainmast. It banked, circled, returned, rolled and rocked its wings, affording the first good sight of its pilot with a leather cap, goggles and white silk scarf. The pilot offered up a salute and a broad smile then suddenly the engine spit and sputtered and the pilot's smile quickly transformed to an expression of serious concern.

The men on the deck watched as the old Jennie climbed and disappeared into the clouds. They watched and heard the engine cough, sputter then die altogether. All grew silent save for the waves striking the ship's hull and the wind in her sails. The silence lingered while all the ship's company watched the sky.

"There! There it is!" shouted a crewman.

Like a silent eagle, the plane emerged from the clouds, seemingly under the control of its pilot until it began to bank, roll, spin and eventually dive, dive, dive, headlong into the sea. The Jennie's wings were torn away violently upon impact with the waves and the fuselage sank almost immediately, its tail fin saluting a final farewell. The ship's company looked on in silence.

"Do we lower a boat, Captain?" asked the First Mate.

Captain Buckmaster looked to the area of the plane's demise where he saw only a few floating remnants of the wings and sadly shook his head.

"No need. There's little we can do for that poor unfortunate bastard," he returned.

Above the ship, unknown to those watching the final pieces of the plane floating about and being swallowed by the sea, a parachute drifted quietly down through the clouds and as those on deck turned away commenting on the cruel death they had just witnessed, a distant voice called out.

"Hey. Hey down there."

None on board heard the cries.

"Hello! Helloooo there!"

Still no one on board the Crimson Glory heard.

"AHOY THERE DAMNIT!"

Then all eyes rose to the voice in the sky where they saw the high-booted, leather clad pilot descending beneath a large old and yellowed silk parachute. Descending not like some well controlled military man or show diver but just plain dropping, fast and furious, and nearly out of control. Just the same the pilot smiled and waved then realizing imminent danger, started to desperately tug at the lines of the parachute.

"Oh shit!" expressed the pilot.

A line snapped loose and the chute started to tear, resulting in a spiraling not so well controlled descent which evolved into a fully out of control spastic experience.

"Oh shit!" repeated the pilot, plunging into the maze of the ship's rigging.

"Oh shit!"

The parachute caught in the rigging, jerking its passenger to a halt high above the deck. As it stretched and settled, the pilot looked around with a smile of relief then suddenly the chute ripped again, gave way and the pilot fell, sliding down the mainsail, bouncing off the mast into a double gainer toward certain death when fortunately the parachute and lines snagged again on some rigging, tossing the pilot around like a yo yo in the hands of a retard. Swaying back and forth in the wind from the roll of the ship, the pilot pulled away an obscuring white scarf and raised the goggles revealing, except for the eyes, a face blackened by oil and smoke. All the ships company of the Crimson Glory stared.

"Well, don't just stand there. Get me outa' this bloody thing!" demanded the pilot.

But, no one moved to help because to their total amazement they realized the pilot… was a woman. Then finally.

"Lend a hand there, men," ordered Captain Buckmaster. "I'll not have it said, Captain Horatio Buckmaster ever let a man… um, pilot, hang from the yardarm of any ship."

The pilot grew a smile but again the smile was quickly lost when above her the old silk parachute ripped, the lines gave way, and down she fell. Bart, with little time to react, simply stretched out his arms to catch her. He missed and she landed heavily on her ass on a large pile of heavy rope where he quickly moved to her aid.

"Are you alright?"

She groaned, sat up painfully, and stared at Bart.

"You're kidding, right mate?"

He helped her up and she inspected her body for broken parts as the men of the ship gathered around, gaping.

Stanley made his way through the crowd to emerge in front of Bart and the pilot who, removing her gloves and continuing to inspect her body, was now, in an obvious Australian accent, expressing her displeasure with the old Jennie biplane.

"Goddamn piece of shit airplane. Gone. All my money, gone. My clothes, gone. Rusty, crab-ridden piece of kangaroo shit. Just wait till I find that son of a bitch who sold…"

She paused when she glanced up to find Stanley and wouldn't you know it, she heard bells, the ship's bell that is as it sounded the watch. Seeing Stanley she suddenly remembered her gender and self-consciously attempted to wipe the oil from her face with her hand then extended it to Stanley.

"Kincade. Roberta Kincade," she smiled. "They call me Bobbie."

Stanley took her hand, not noticing the gunk from her face he'd contracted in the process.

"Wellington. Stanley Wellington," he returned.

Bart stepped up and extended his hand as well.

"Haile," he said. "Bart Haile."

Still focused on Stanley she was oblivious of his gesture. The Red Baron had shot Bart down again.

A short time later Stanley and the Captain entered the crew's mess to find their newly arrived pilot, Bobbie, sitting at a table, still black faced and the center of attraction, surrounded by the rugby boys. She slapped the table as she delivered the punch line to what must have been a great story and brought all the boys to laughter.

"So, you've been flying since you were ten years old?" asked Chrisfield.

"Hold on there, mate. Where I come from you don't ask a lady questions until you've been properly introduced," snapped Bobbie.

Eager to please, all the boys started introducing themselves at the same time resulting in a confused scramble of chatter until the room was silenced with a brief whistle and there stood Jonesy who then handed Bobbie a hot cup of coffee.

"You'll have to excuse my friends, ma'am," Jonesy apologized. "They're all uncultured Princeton jocks. However, not to be rude, I'll be happy to introduce them."

Jonesy pulled his large wooden spoon from his apron and started from left to right, pointing as he went with the spoon. The boys offered varied forms of bows and tweaks as their names were called.

"Lewis Collier, Bradley Harrington, Bart Haile, Mule Van Horn, James Franklin, Oscar Lynch, Big Tiny Braxton, Geoffrey Chrisfield, Stuart MacMullen, Kicker Stevens, Artie Lambert, Henry Vickers, Edward Cross, and… Stinky."

"Just Stinky?" inquired Bobbie.

"You don't want to know, ma'am," answered Big Tiny.

Stinky stood and bowed to shake hands with Bobbie but he was yanked back and held by Edward who pulled his watch cap down over his face.

"Don't be embarrassing the lady now, Stinky," he laughed.

"And you are?" Bobbie asked of Jonesy.

"My name is Soo," replied the cordial cook.

"Sue?"

Big Tiny snickered and Jonesy shot him a wooden spoon warning.

"Soo Lee Min Jones, ma'am. Rhodes Scholar, Oxford, twenty-seven. And ship's chef."

"Chef," laughed Bart.

Jonesy again threatened with the deadly spoon then turned back to Bobbie.

"My friends call me…"

"Shorty," interrupted Bart, raising laughter from around the table.

"Jonesy, ma'am," said Jonesy, trying desperately to ignore their sophomoric antics. "Just call me Jonesy."

"And I'm Captain Horatio Buckmaster."

They all looked up to discover the Captain and Stanley who had just entered.

"Gentlemen, baring any more… surprises, we should be reaching our destination by nightfall," said the Captain. "We all have work to do and I'm sure our guest would like to get cleaned up."

"Irish is waiting in the cargo hold, gents," added Stanley, thumbing over his shoulder toward the door.

The rugby boys departed the mess, some shaking Bobbie's hand along the way. Stanley nodded for Bart to stay, the both of them joining Bobbie at the table while Captain Buckmaster casually leaned against a post.

"Mrs. Kincade, I'm afraid…"

That's Miss Kincade and it's quite all right, Captain. I understand. No place for a woman here and all that. You can dump me at the first port of convenience."

"Quite the contrary, Miss Kincade. I was about to tell you that there is no convenient port. We are bound for… well, not a place you might wish to be discharged."

"Oh. And that is?"

The Captain looked to Stanley then continued with a suggestion.

"However, there is an island of amiable population three days sail southwest of here. But that would be the decision of the ship's owner."

"And who would that be?" asked Bobbie.

"Mr. Wellington here," replied the Captain.

Stanley looked to the Captain, "Amiable. Just how amiable, Captain?"

Captain Buckmaster answered with a slight nod of disapproval. Stanley then turned back to Bobbie.

"Well, Miss Kincade..."

"Bobbie," she corrected.

"Bobbie. You're more than welcome to stay with us until you can gain better circumstances," he offered, looking again to the Captain. "No harm I suppose. As long as she stays on board."

The Captain nodded agreement, knowing very well there was no other choice in the matter. Bobbie looked from one to the other and to a silent Bart.

"Yanks, right?" she asked.

Bart smiled and nodded a yes.

"Say, you're not smugglers are you?"

Bart laughed and nodded a no.

"Slavers?"

Again Bart nodded a no.

"Pirates," she questioned further. "Some of your boys looked pretty beat up like they've been up to some kind of mischief."

"You might say they have but I assure you, you're quite safe with us, Miss Kincade. As long as you stay about the ship," answered Captain Buckmaster, turning to Bart and continuing. "Mr. Haile, would you be so kind as to find our guest some quarters and a more suitable wardrobe?"

"Sure thing, Skipper," acknowledged Bart. "Come along Bobbie."

Bart hopped up and exited the crews mess followed

by Bobbie who looked back just before leaving.

"Nice of you, Mr. Wellington," she said. "For a Yank."

Stanley smiled in return then asked, "Oh, by the way. What were you doing flying out here in the middle of nowhere anyway?"

"Crashing," smiled Bobbie.

Bart was leading Bobbie along the passageway to her cabin when she offered the first bit of conversation.

"Nice boys, that bunch. Princeton, eh."

"Yep," confirmed Bart.

"What's that?"

"What's what?" returned Bart.

"Princeton."

"Princeton? Oh, it's a home for the chronically auspicious."

"Oh," replied Bobbie. "Say mate, that Wellington fellah is kind of cryptic isn't he."

"Stanley? Nah, not really. Just got things on his mind."

"Oh yeah. Like what?" she questioned.

"Um… stuff. You know. Big things," answered Bart, then whispering to himself, "Like getting us all killed."

"What? Afraid I didn't catch that."

Bart stopped at the door of her cabin and opened it.

"Well'p, here you are. Home sweet home. I'll dig up some duds for you. Anything else you need just ring for the butler."

"Butler?"

"Just kidding."

Bobbie watched as Bart moved off down the passageway, shrugged her shoulders and turned to enter the small cabin. As she did she saw across the small room a mirror and in the mirror the oil and smoke smeared face of a stranger. She then realized the stranger was herself resulting in a hastily blurted, "Oh shit."

chapter 9

The ship rolled easily and majestically through the Indian Ocean toward the sunset as though it knew its only purpose was the safe passage of all aboard. She was dependable and forgiving as the Captain had told Stanley back in New York and she had certainly proved it on this journey.

Bobbie emerged on deck from below and looked about. The light of a nearby lamp illuminated her face and it could easily be seen the oil smudged tomboy pilot had transformed into an attractive woman in spite of the borrowed men's clothing. She looked to find Jonesy perched on top a cargo hatch doing his nightly Tae Chi then spied Bart stretched out against a mast and she strolled over.

"Hello there, mate."

Bart perked up.

"Oh, hi. Say, you look just like a girl. I mean… well you know."

Bobbie offered a gracious smile then looked over to Jonesy.

"What's that, some kind of religious thing?"

Bart sat up and looked over to Jonesy who appeared almost in a trance as he moved in a strange but graceful slow motion mix of ballet and martial arts.

"Oh no. That's just Jonesy," he replied.

"Right, but what's he doing?"

Bart looked again for a brief moment and realized he had no damn idea.

"Oh, he calls that Tight Cheese or something. Um, something about universal enlightenment and um, rheumatism. Yeah, that's it."

She watched Jonesy, framed by the grand ship and an incredible Sunset, perform his Tae Chi perfectly. It was a tranquil and quiet scene filled only with the music of straining lines in the ship's rigging and the creaking of her wooden soul.

"You know, it's awfully nice of Mr. Wellington to take me in like this," she told Bart.

"Don't think he had much choice. You did kind of just… drop in."

"I guess I did at that. Still, I'm extremely grateful."

"Well, maybe you should tell him," suggested Bart, throwing a thumb over his shoulder. "He doesn't bite. At least not lately."

She looked up to see Stanley standing alone near the wheel house looking out over the sea and went to join him.

"My father used to do that," she said as she came up behind him.

"Oh, good evening," greeted Stanley as he turned. "Your father?"

"Stare out into nowhere," she explained.

Stanley nodded understanding.

"I asked him once what he was doing and he said he was looking at the future."

"And what future was that?"

"I don't know. He died soon after. A plane crash. He was a pilot."

"Oh, sorry," said Stanley, trying but failing to distinguish the color of Bobbies eyes in the dim light. "So he was a pilot. Like you."

"Better I hope," she laughed then stood there for an uncomfortable silent moment.

Stanley nodded agreement, wanting to say something but failing to do so.

"You've all been very kind, Mr. Wellington. I'm grateful."

"Stanley. Please call me Stanley."

He pulled out his cigarette case, offered one to Bobbie and after her decline withdrew and lit one for himself. Since going to sea he had aborted the silver cigarette holder, deeming it too pretentious and troublesome.

"I'm surprised," said Bobbie.

"At what?"

"That you haven't pried. About who I am and why I'm here, I mean."

"None of my business. I figure you'd tell us if you wanted to."

"It's your ship. You have a right to know."

They both turned and looked out to sea, enjoying the sunset.

"My grandfather once said it's a vast ocean and everything on it and about it comes and goes in its own time. I'm still not sure what that means but I figure it applies to people as well."

"Funny, you don't impress me as the romantic philosophical kind," observed Bobbie. "More the lawyer type."

"In time," laughed Stanley. "So, were you actually trying to get somewhere?" he continued. "Or is crashing into the ocean just a casual past-time?"

"My father had a number of his own planes. Used to run cargo in and out of Sydney. After he died I took over the business but some nasty competitors tried to shut me down."

Stanley turned and studied her face as she told her story. He found himself more than pleased with what he saw.

"It wasn't hard to figure out my father's death was no accident. They found out I knew and came after me too so I took one of the planes and left the country. Only so much a girl can do against a determined bunch like that, you know."

"And that's it?" asked Stanley, feeling there had to be more.

"Well, not quite. I kinda'… damaged their planes before I left," she revealed, slightly embarrassed.

"Damaged?"

"Um. Blew them up, actually."

"You mean boom! Just blew them up?"

"Yeah, pretty much. Six of them actually," she smiled. "They caught up with me though. In New Guinea. They stole my father's plane but I got away. Then I bought that old Jennie and… well, here I am."

"You just… blew them up?" repeated Stanley.

Bobbie smiled and nodded confirmation, generating a smile in return from Stanley. The moment was interrupted when they heard Jonesy begin ranting in Chinese and turned to see him, frustrated, trying unsuccessfully to teach Bart how to do Tae Chi. Bart somehow managed to tie himself into a knot and fall on his ass.

"I hear Bart's a bit of a genius," commented Bobbie.

"Kind of. He's got a photographic memory. Reads fast and remembers everything," laughed Stanley. "But he runs on emotion which makes for quite a combination."

"Is that good or bad?"

"Enviable," observed Stanley, looking down on Bart

with affection. "Enviable."

Suddenly a long awaited announcement rose from the foredeck watch.

"Land ho! Island ahead!"

A number of crewman quickly emerged from below decks to gain their first look at their storied mysterious destination. Bart and Jonesy stood tall on the cargo hatch eagerly joined by an excited Chrisfield. Captain Buckmaster, who had been lingering in the wheelhouse throughout the evening with expectations of soon reaching their destination, exited and began barking orders.

"Soundings! Quickly there! Soundings!" He then called, "First Mate!"

"Aye Skipper?"

"Let's take in some sail. Take her slow," he ordered.

"Aye Skipper," replied the First Mate who turned and began sending men aloft.

The hurried voices of crewmen could be heard all about the ship and the entire ship's company lit up with excitement.

"Be ready to let loose the anchor!" called the Captain.

"Aye Capt'n," came the reply.

The profile of the island came through the evening's failing light. As they neared, the depth readings became adequate to drop anchor.

"Away anchor!" yelled Captain Buckmaster.

"Anchor away!" replied a crewman as the anchor

slipped down into the sea, its chains rattling speedily until it came to rest on the bottom.

Captain Buckmaster turned and looked to Stanley with a bit of concern.

"Well young Wellington. It seems your map was correct after all," he observed. "Now, I wonder as to the rest of the story."

Stanley looked to the Captain then to Bart and smiled. Bart returned the smile nervously then turned to view the island. An eerie mist seemed to engulf much of its night gray green tones but a bright rising moon was enough to reveal steamy jungle covered mountains and a prominent smoldering volcano. The old sailor came to mind.

"Perdition," whispered Bart.

chapter 10

Bobbie awoke to the sounds of a busy ship and heavy feet vibrating through the bulkhead. Men conversed loudly as they shuffled and banged equipment around topside, others were yelling up from below in the cargo hold. When she sat up in her birth the conversation of two crewmen walking in the passageway drifted in through the louvered door of her cabin.

"Sure I heard tell of this place once. Now I ain't spunkless but I swear it'd take the threat of my mother's own life to get me on that island."

"Oh hell man, you really believe all that whisky bar bilge?"

Bobbie rose, opened the door slightly and peeked out to see the two crewmen as they continued through the ship.

"Ain't sayin' I do and ain't sayin' I don't. But stories like that don't carry long what they ain't got some truth is what I'm sayin'."

"Well I don't hold to it. To damn crazy to be true."

"Just the same. I ain't goin' ashore less it's the Skipper's orders and so far he ain't ordered."

"Don't matter much anyway. As I understand it, it's them college boys that's going ashore. Don't know what for. They been kind of tight lipped about it the whole damn voyage."

"Tight lipped you calls it. Scared I calls it. You seen all them guns? Ain't no picnic those boys is headin' to. Not in this part of the world."

Bobbie closed the cabin door and quickly began to dress. Minutes later she arrived on deck to discover a bee hive of activity. A launch was being lowered and another was being loaded with various kinds gear. As she moved closer to the action she was surprised to see all the friendly college boys were now packing .45 automatic pistols, some on the hip and others in shoulder holsters. Most were sporting bandoleers of ammunition, and additional weapons were being loaded in the boats. It was a sight she hadn't expected and with a simple change of hats the Princeton rugby boys could easily pass for a band of Poncho Villa's finest.

Irish was leaning over the side of the ship supervising the lowering of the launch.

"Level there, mates! Level off now. Right. Right.

Now you've got her."

Irish glanced over and saw Stinky who was getting ready to toss what looked like an oversized backpack to Big Tiny standing in the launch. He rushed over and grabbed the pack, surprising Stinky, then offered a nervous smile.

"Easy there, boyo," said Irish. "Not to be overly concerned, laddie, but this here's a flamethrower pack. You can't be tossin' it around like you do that rugby ball. And I'm sure your mum ain't prayin' to the saints for her baby ta come home like an over cooked pork pie."

Bobbie inspected some of the cargo going into the launch and discovered varied weapons including a case of dynamite. She then looked up to find Stanley standing next to her.

"Good morning," he said with a smile.

"Oh, morning," she returned. "Nice day for a war isn't it."

"Just a little expedition," laughed Stanley. "Exploring, actually."

"Exploring?"

"Yes."

"For what?"

"Um, rocks."

"Rocks?" she asked.

"Yes. Excuse me," he said as he moved off and entered into an unheard conversation with Irish. Bobbie strolled along until she met up with Bart.

"Morning."

"Morning," returned Bart.

"Expecting trouble are we?" she asked.

Bart offered up his signature shit-eating smile, "Nah, just… being careful. You know. Wild pigs and things."

"Pigs."

"Right. Excuse me," said Bart as he skipped off to help Mule lift and load a case of ammunition. Big Tiny received the case and secured it in the launch.

"Alright, that's it," he yelled up to the crew. "Lower her down."

He held fast to the line at the bow of the boat and rode it down to the water. Bobbie, backing away from the action, bumped into Captain Buckmaster.

"Careful there, Miss. Kincade. Ship's doings here abouts."

She smiled sheepishly and followed him as he walked to meet Stanley.

"I'm thinking it might be a good idea to bring along Jonesy. His language skills might come in handy in case we meet some natives," suggested Stanley.

Captain Buckmaster nodded agreement and turned to a nearby crewman.

"You there. Go below and fetch Jonesy for the shore party," he ordered.

"And we could use one or two more good men."

The Captain turned to find the two crewmen Bobbie heard talking earlier in the passageway. One of the crewmen was about to object before the Captain could get out the words.

"Captain, I..."

Then Bobbie jumped in, saving him the effort.

"I'll go," she quickly volunteered.

Captain Buckmaster immediately began to object.

"Miss. Kincade, I hardly think..."

She moved past the Captain and straight to Stanley.

"I'm quite handy with a gun."

Stanley hesitated, surprised by the request. Bart was nearby and shook his head no. Everyone paused, waiting for Stanley's decision, fully expecting him to refuse. She moved closer and spoke to Stanley in confidence.

"I can blow shit up," she said with a smile.

"Well... alright. But you stay with me or the Captain here. And do what you're told."

Bart rolled his eyes and turned away. "I knew it," he mumbled. "I knew he couldn't say no to a skirt. What a softy."

The Crimson Glory's two launches were rowed in and landed on a small beach set between two high cliffs and large outcroppings. As the shore party disembarked they looked about and discovered the tall rock cliffs formed an impenetrable crescent that horseshoed the entire beach.

"Secure those launches," ordered Captain Buckmaster. "And I want one of you crewmen to stay with them."

Stanley moved ahead of the others, looking around until he made an odd discovery. Crushed and wedged

into a crevasse high up in the side of a cliff was a launch
not unlike their own but decades older and it was easy to
construe the boat's circumstances could not have been
brought about by natural causes. He was soon joined by
the rest of the company who were now suited up with
gear and weapons. They stared up in silence at the boat,
none venturing to guess how it could have gotten there.
Then they suddenly recoiled when a mass of screaming
sea birds burst into flight from within and behind the old
wreck where they were nesting. Stanley collected
himself after seeing the ghostly sight and turned to the
men.

"Spread out," he ordered. "Look for a way over these
cliffs."

As they all wandered off, Stanley turned for another
look at the derelict boat, trying to imagine what kind of
natural force could have put it there.

"Needs a little work I'd say," observed Bart, as he
handed Stanley his gear.

"Yeah, just a bit," agreed Stanley.

They were joking words but neither of them was
laughing.

"Over here!" they heard Stuart yell from further up
the beach.

They turned and saw Stuart moving up a dune hill
and quickly followed. When they came over the crest of
the dune they found a steep stairway carved into the rock
face which rose about three hundred feet to eventually
enter into what appeared to be a hole in the side of the

cliff. Stanley looked to Captain Buckmaster.

"Well, Mr. Wellington it's your shore party," said the Captain. "Shall we continue?"

He looked to the eager group then up to the cliff, turned and began the climb. The others shifted their packs, secured their weapons and followed, eventually becoming a single line procession strung out from the base of the cliff to the top of the steps where Stanley had just arrived.

The dark entrance at the top of the steep climb turned out to be a tunnel through which Stanley could see light filtering in from the other end. He paused, looked down at the rest of the ascending shore party then turned and entered.

Eventually emerging from the tunnel into the light, Stanley looked out and immediately froze, awestruck. He was joined by Bart, Bobbie and the Captain, each reacting with similar silent surprise at what they saw. Spreading before them in a lush valley below lay a great city in ruins; its unfamiliar architecture part of a culture and civilization long lost to all recorded history. Beyond the city, standing higher than all the other dilapidated splendid stone structures stood a great wall. Nowhere could there be seen any sign of life.

"You think anybody's home," Bobbie asked of Bart.

"I hope not," he replied.

Below them were more stairs carved into the hillside that lead down into the valley. Stanley wasted no time and began the descent followed by the other three. Little

Jonesy and Big Tiny were the next to emerge from the tunnel to discover the awesome sight and they're reaction was much the same.

"Holy shit!" exclaimed Jonesy, in Chinese.

"What?" asked Big Tiny.

Jonesy didn't bother to translate his words. He was already eagerly heading down the steps leading to the deserted ancient city.

chapter 11

The group entered the city carefully, looking about at the overgrown ghostly ruins and trying to imagine a time when it was prosperous and teeming with people. They made their way along what must have once been the main thoroughfare and came to stop in a central plaza, removed their packs, sat and rested.

"Looks like a good base camp," said Stanley as he turned to Captain Buckmaster for endorsement. "Captain?"

"Good as any I suppose," he replied. "But where do we go from here?"

"Not sure," replied Stanley. "I guess we have to first figure out where here is."

"Here is nowhere, remember?" said Bart. "We're in an uncharted city on an uncharted island and nobody's home. So, can we go back to Princeton now? I don't like the looks of this neighborhood."

Stanley sat on the steps of what was once a large impressive stone structure now reduced to a shell of rubble. He pulled out his canteen and the map and while taking a swig of water was joined by Bart and Chrisfield.

Bart removed his pack as he settled on the steps next to him then leaned over and expressed in a confidential whisper, "That old sailor never said anything about this."

"No he didn't," replied Stanley with a slight hint of concern.

"This place reminds me of someone I read about once," said Chrisfield. "This guy who took up anthropology and developed a theory that the entire Pacific Rim was populated from the descendants of an ancient race of highly advanced people. When he presented his theory to the scientific community they all said he was nuts and turned him away."

"Makes sense," said Bart. "Everything's got to start somewhere, right? So what did the guy do?"

"He swore he would prove his theory. Went out and found some old rich guy to finance an expedition then he went off in search of evidence," answered Chrisfield. "Now can you imagine that? Some old rich guy being crazy enough to pay for an expedition to who knows where based on a whim and a prayer?"

"Yeah, kind of ludicrous isn't it?" said Bart, looking at Stanley. "So what happened? Did he prove his theory?"

"Nope. Heard he got captured and eaten by cannibals on some island in Malaysia or somewhere," answered Chrisfield as he sprawled heavily on the steps and looked about. "I wonder what happened to the people who lived here?"

Bart looked around at the ruins with no clue whatsoever as to the demise of the city's former residents but offered up with academic authority a theory just the same. "Died quietly of old age. I hope."

While the others rested, Bobbie wandered about, rounded a large pile of downed columns that looked as though they may once have adorned the equivalent of a city hall then walking clear of the obstructing view, she looked off beyond the end of the grand avenue and saw in the distance the massive high wall. She was joined by Jonesy and for a brief moment they were both speechless as they observed and thoughtfully wondered about its origin.

"Holy shit," mumbled Jonesy, in Chinese.

"Looks bigger than the Great Wall of China, wouldn't you think, Jonesy?" asked Bobbie.

"Wouldn't know. I'm from Fresno. But I wouldn't bet against it."

"Yeah, well somebody sure as hell did and it looks like they lost the bet."

The great towering stone wall structure was overrun and dripping with various vegetation. Incorporated into the wall was what appeared to have been a huge gate, larger than any first impression would deem practical or useful for any civilization, past or present. The gate was constructed of layers of extremely thick vertical wood timbers now hanging in rot and ruin but preserved enough to demonstrate its original design and to show that it was apparently destroyed in a violent manner as though it had been rammed by a rolling boulder the size and power of a battle ship. It crossed Bobbie's mind there were no man made land mobile machines capable of producing such results, not even in the modern industrial time of 1933.

While Bobbie and Jonesy were studying the distant wall they suddenly heard something dart in and out of the shadows of the nearby ruins behind them. They turned about quickly and a brief moment later it again darted from one shadow to another. Bobbie looked expectantly to Jonesy.

"Well?" she said.

"No thanks. I don't chase anything bigger than me," replied Jonesy.

"Well that includes just about everything, eh mate," she observed.

She shook her head in disappointment, pulled her .45 out of its holster, cocked it, looked back to the source of disturbance in the ruins and started in to investigate. Just then something leaped out of the shadows with a yelp like a wild creature. Coming face to face with Bobbie and the pistol it quickly turned and darted through the piles of rubble to hurdle a large section of a downed column. From the other side of the column popped up

Big Tiny who snatched the little creature like it was a passed rugby ball. The creature shrieked, bit Big Tiny on the hand and gaining its freedom quickly turned to escape only to find it was surrounded by the rugby boys.

Irish made his way to the circle and observed, "Well, I'll be buggered. And all this time I been thinkin' t'was only we Irish who was cursed with the pesky little people."

They all stared curiously at what appeared to be a scruffy little native boy who commenced to direct some sort of unintelligible verbal abuse on Irish.

"I think you just might have insulted the lad," said Mule.

"That little turd bit me," came an angry Big Tiny.

Stanley, Bart and the Captain joined the circle next to Big Tiny who was now nursing his minor injury and broken pride with sympathy and self pity. Bart looked at the small boy then at Big Tiny, shook his head and snickered. Bobbie and Jonesy came and completed the circle. Jonesy looked to the small boy then to Big Tiny and shook his head with a chuckle. Big Tiny then decided he would tolerate no more humiliation and slapped Jonesy on the back of the head, sending his hat rolling into the circle.

"Jonesy, see if you can pick up on his lingo," suggested Stanley.

Jonesy retrieved his hat and approached the boy. The boy stepped back. Then Jonesy held out his hands to show friendship.

"Um… say something kid,' said Jonesy.

The frightened but feisty little native boy looked at Jonesy then gave him a well practiced up yours Sicilian salute.

Jonesy is of course taken aback and turns to Stanley. "I believe he just said…"

"Boy, do you understand what we say?" Stanley interrupted.

The boy simply stared.

"We're not going to hurt you. Do you understand?" continued Stanley who then turned to Jonesy for assistance. "Well Jonesy?"

"Mr. Wellington, I can't understand what he says unless he actually says something."

"Well… try something."

Jonesy turned back to the boy and thought a moment, then, "Hey kid. Your father's a bilge rat and your mother wears combat boots."

The boy's eyes turned to fire, he growled, lowered his head and shot into Jonesy's gut like a Rocky Mountain ram, sending him back on his ass at Big Tiny's feet. Big Tiny looked down, shook his head and chuckled.

"You no talk on my mother! She damn good fun time bitch!" blurted the boy.

They all stared in disbelief at hearing the boy's words, including Big Tiny while he easily lifted little Jonesy to his feet with one hand. Jonesy brushed himself off and moved to Stanley's side.

"I believe he said…"

"I know what he said," came Stanley as he turned to the boy. "Where are your people? Where do you live? How do you know our language? What do you call this place?"

"Hey, slow down there, chief," suggested Bart. "I don't think the kid's got his doctorate degree yet."

"Oh, right," said Stanley, catching himself.

The boy looked to Stanley, "Chief. You Chief?"

Stanley looked to the group, then shrugged his shoulders, "Well, um… yes. Wellington. Chief Wellington. What's your name?"

"Me Ikohuliatamolu Shit Head. Son of son of Sailorman Shit Head. Father Shit Head number two, son of Sailorman Shit Head. I know sailor talk. Father teach. Father learn from Sailorman Shit Head number one. Father say, his father, Sailorman Shit Head number one, leave island long time. No come back. He say, Sailorman Shit Head and other sailormans make big trouble with Myuko. Many people die. Father say sailormans not good come again. Get Myuko all fuckin' pissed off. He say Sailorman Shit Head better off he stay goddamn oceanside."

"Ah, the universal language of the sea," observed Bart.

"Yeah, sounds like this sailorman fellah had a limited vocabulary," expressed Jonesy.

"Boy, you take…" began Stanley.

"I Ikohuliatamolu Shit Head. Son of…"

"I know, I know. I think we'll just call you Boy. It's a good name," said Stanley.

Bart looked to Stanley who simply shrugged his shoulders.

"Hey, it worked for Tarzan," he smiled then approached the boy and going down on one knee he asked. "Boy, take us to…"

Bart couldn't believe what he was about to hear. He rolled his eyes and cleared his throat hoping to prevent Stanley's delivery of a classic corny line. He failed.

"Boy, take us to your leader," Stanley continued.

"All people down under," answered Boy.

"What?"

"People down under."

"What? You mean your people went to Australia and left you here alone? You poor little thing," sympathized Bobbie.

"People down under," Boy repeated, pointing to the ground and searching for the appropriate words.

"I think he means they're all dead," suggested Chrisfield. "People down under. Stay from light. Stay from light time when come… what Sailorman Shit Head call… Bad Coons."

"Bad what?" asked Bart.

"Bad Coons," repeated Boy.

The boy pantomimes the creatures he's speaking of by doing a vicious monkey dance. Bart joined the charade and did his own little monkey dance along with some verbalization.

"Whoo whoo whoo," said Bart.

"Yes. Bad Coons," agreed Boy.

Upon understanding, Bart ceased his monkey act, "Oh, you mean monkeys. Baboons," suggest Bart.

"Yes. Bab… Bab Coons."

Bart rose with a broad smile, "Well, that's a relief. So much for the monster ape theory."

"Hurry, we go now. You meet father, Chief Shit Head."

Stanley turned to the group, "Well, you heard the kid. We go now. Meet Chief… Shit Head."

The shore party was led by the boy through the city, parading as relaxed as a tour group or overconfident soldiers on patrol somewhere safe well behind the enemy lines. Jonesy looked over to Bart and couldn't resist a little ribbing.

"Whoo whoo whoo," Jonesy laughed.

Bart brushed him off with a wave.

"I must admit that's one language I have yet to master," laughed Jonesy.

Kicker joined in the fun with another, "Whoo whoo whoo."

Jonesy couldn't resist a repeat, "Whoo whoo whoo."

Soon the other rugby boys were all in on the gag.

"Whoo whoooo," came Lewis.

"Whoo whoo whoo," came Bradley.

"Whoooo whoooo whoooo," laughed Big Tiny.

"No, no!" said Boy as he stopped and turned, growing extremely concerned. His senses sharpened as he searched the perimeter.

There came another whoo whoo whoo and Bart looked to the group.

"Hey come on. Knock it off, fellahs," demanded Bart.

They shook their heads and shrugged as though to say it ain't us. Then it came again.

"Whoo whoo."

And again, "Whoo whoo whoo."

Then suddenly it started coming from all around them and from all directions, louder and louder, "Whoo whoo whoo."

Boy's eyes grew wide and desperate as he looked all around then turned quickly to the Crimson Glory column.

"Bad Coons!" he yelled. "Bad Coons!"

The boy sprinted off like some little delinquent who just got sighted by the principal smoking cigarettes behind the gymnasium, all the while calling back to the group.

"Sailormans run! Come quick! Run!"

Instead of them heeding Boy's warnings they simply stood about looking to the sounds coming from within the surrounding ruins. Then came a loud echoing, whoo whoo whoo whaaaaah! And out of the ruins emerged half a dozen long-snouted, long fanged, long haired, wild eyed, screaming, oversized, near man sized baboons. At first they offered only noisy intimidation as they edged toward the shore party then they were joined by a dozen others from everywhere among the surrounding old city. The shore party silently and nervously readied their weapons. The only one offering to comment on their situation being little Jonesy.

"Holy shit!" he exclaimed, in Chinese.

Boy, still running, looked back to find the group hadn't followed. He stopped, threw up his arms then started back to them calling, "Sailormans run! RUN!"

Behind him a wild-eyed baboon, easily twice the boy's size or bigger, leaped to the ground in pursuit. It then leaped through the air, intent on ripping out the boy's throat with its deadly fangs when suddenly a shot thundered through the ruins of the old city and the would be killer baboon's head exploded as it fell to the ground. Boy froze, looked to the dead baboon then to Stanley with a smile of gratitude but his smile quickly changed to fear when he warned and pointed to Stanley's rear. With smoking .45 in hand, he was turned around by a horrid animal scream just in time to blast another baboon as it lunged forward. At the same moment the other members of the group opened fire in defense from the onrush of killer creatures.

A round-eyed Bart brought his rifle to bear just in time to blow away one of the ugly attackers but had no time to aim again and instead butted another beast across the head. He desperately pulled his .45 and finished the job. Another charged and met the same fate. Bart nervously shot, stepped back, shot, stepped back, and shot again. Each shot being lethal not because he was an expert marksman but because his targets were deadpan close.

"This is crazy!" he said nervously with each shot. "This is crazy! This is crazy!"

Stanley was now shooting with two .45's and found no shortage of targets as he ran to meet Boy and put him behind him for protection. The beasts kept coming from all directions.

Bobbie and Jonesy found themselves back to back with Bobbie expending accurate expert rapid fire with a repeater rifle while little Jonesy, having snatched the elephant gun from one of the rugby boys, seemed dwarfed by its presence. Just then a particularly large, ugly, nasty creature charged straight for him. He struggled to hold steady the heavy weapon then managed to fire at the last second sending the ugly critter careening backward in assorted pieces, the force of the blast knocking both he and Bobbie to the ground. Bobbie recovered and looked up just in time to blast another bad coon, which, having launched itself from the top of a standing column seemed to have somehow just dropped out of the sky.

The other members of the group were all in similar circumstance, shooting repeatedly while being swarmed by the would-be killers from all directions, terrifying creatures attacking without fear or any sense of peril. Big Tiny was forced to converted his bazooka to a baseball bat, swinging left then right then left again, clomping a creature with each effort. As they fell dazed to the ground, Chrisfield chopped them up with a Thompson machine gun.

It was a hellish hectic mess with bloody baboons falling and being cut to pieces everywhere in rapid fire mayhem. It was Custer at the Little Big Horn except this time the only thing the Indians were armed with were big yellow teeth and a lot of attitude. As the battle continued, the human element fought its way into a defensive circle, taking shelter among the ruins, all the while expending a continuous barrage of fire until finally the screaming baboons were defeated. In the subsequent silence the group stood in total post battle adrenaline shock, surveying the bloody mess that was once a small army of wild lethal creatures. The silence was broken when suddenly one of the baboons screamed and started to rise. Irish responded quickly with a shot to the head then all was quiet on the ruin front once again.

"Everybody all right?" asked Captain Buckmaster.

They began checking themselves as though they hadn't had time to notice if they were injured, bleeding or even dead. Then from within the ruins came another whoo whoo whoo and up popped the second wave, more than the first, moving, positioning, approaching carefully and this time, above all the rest rose Big Daddy Bad Coon himself, bigger, uglier and nastier than all the rest. He was older and heavily scared from years of defending his rule from challenging young males. Big Daddy climbed to the highest position he could find, snarled down at the group and locked eyes with Stanley. Stanley stared back as if accepting the challenge, as though he had any choice, then quickly reloaded his weapons.

"Take out that big bastard first," said Stanley. "He must be the leader. Maybe it'll steal their thunder and we can run for it."

Bart looked to Stanley as if to say you gotta' be kiddin'. "Crazy," he mumbled nervously. "Crazy."

"Holy shit," said a very nervous Jonesy. In Chinese.

Stanley shrugged and offered him a reassuring smile.

Big Daddy Bad Coon snarled, his long threatening sharp yellow fangs seeming to grow with his anger. He growled and started to order the attack with a whoo whoo whoooo when suddenly from far beyond the wall, echoing off the mountains deep in the jungle came an incredibly horrendous ROAR! All the advancing baboons froze, some even cowered, and they all looked to Big Daddy for guidance. Big Daddy Bad Coon turned and looked to the jungle beyond the great wall then turned back to once again lock eyes with Stanley. He let loose a threatening scream then turned and disappeared into the ruins. The remaining baboon army took his cue and quickly melted away into the shadows of the ancient city. The shore party stood silent and perplexed until Boy regained their focus.

"Now sailormans run?"

No reply was offered. None was necessary. They quickly checked their weapons, gathered their gear, and with a newfound heightened awareness moved off sharply behind Boy.

chapter 12

When the expedition finally reached the edge of the ancient city Boy led them into a dense canopy of old trees where they arrived at a large carved stone figurehead. The primitive head was a grotesque rendition of some kind of monkey which all in the party readily assumed to be a baboon. It was partially overgrown and covered with the roots of a huge tropical tree easily hundreds of years old and had a large mouth three times the size of Big Tiny. The mouth apparently served as an entrance to somewhere and was sealed by a boulder on which was carved the teeth. Boy stopped and pointed to the big ugly head.

"Down under," he said.

"Oh great," mumbled Bart.   "Here comes the

perdition part."

Stanley went to the boulder, gave it a shove and discovered it wouldn't move. Big Tiny, Bradley and Oscar joined in the effort alternately shoving and pushing in various directions but still the boulder wouldn't budge.

"Okay Boy, what's the secret?" asked Stanley who found the boy missing when he turned.

"Sailormans come," directed Boy who had quietly climbed up and was now standing near the tree above the large head. "Sailormans come up down under."

"What's with this kid?" asked Bart of no one in particular. "Up down under? We gotta' go up to go down to meet somebody named Shit Head. What's next, the Mad Hatter and the White Rabbit?"

"Where's that man of faith and courage?" Stanley asked of Bart, laughing as he began to climb up the tree roots to join Boy."

"A million miles east of here where I left him after I choked on that damn cigar."

"Don't worry, mate," Bobbie assured Bart as she followed Stanley. "Whoever this Shit Head is he can't be any uglier than this fellah here," she said, referring to the sculpted stone head.

"Right," Bart agreed, uncomfortably studying the size of the primitive carved primate likeness.

"Whoo whoo whoo," kidded Mule as he patted Bart on the back and started to climb.

When they had all ascended the big ugly head and

were gathered together at the top Boy turned to the extremely wide old tree and gave it a hardy kick. The thick bark separated and became a door; which popped open enough for Boy to grab and pull it open further after which he pointed to a dark hole in the hollow opening.

"Down under," he said.

Stanley entered the tree carefully and discovered a ladder leading down into the darkness.

"Down under," he said smiling back to Bart.

"Perdition," mumbled Bart. "No place for a lawyer. Not till he's dead anyhow."

When the group came down the ladder they found themselves in a tunnel which extended far into the darkness. Stanley struck a match and looked around to discover a number of torches stacked in an old urn. He lit one and handed it to Henry then another and held it up for a better view. Boy was the last to descend the ladder. He weaved through the group quickly and scooted away, knowing the tunnel well enough not to need the light of the torches.

"Sailormans come."

"Some poor bugger spent a lot of time and sweat cutting out this hole in God's earth," observed Irish as they moved out to follow the boy.

"No one did, actually," replied Chrisfield. "It's natural."

"It don't look natural to me, laddie."

"It's a lava tube," explained Chrisfield. "Old. Maybe

thousands of year old."

"A what?"

"Lava tube. Created by the flow of volcanic molten rock. Flowed through like a malt shop straw then cooled and hardened."

"Hot then cold then empty and hard," said Irish. "I knew a woman like that once."

After nearly twenty minutes they came to hear the distant sound of drums echoing through the tunnel. As they moved along the drums grew louder. When Boy eventually led them into the light they were surprised to discover a large village with hundreds of native residents. The village contained all the expected attributes such as gardens, tropical grass huts, a large communal hootch, cooking fires, and more. The attentions of most members of the shore party were drawn to the sites of the village. Chrisfield however was drawn more to the village surroundings, the natural formations, and looked up and around.

"I'll be damned. It's a volcano. We're inside a dormant volcano." he observed.

Chrisfield's observation was correct. The village was situated in a large volcanic bowl that made up the natives protected world. The rim rose high and surrounded them on all sides except for a limited opening at one side of about fifty yards that functioned like a huge picture window. Beyond the opening was the ocean.

Perceiving no immediate threat, the members of the expedition began to spread out, absorbing the sight of their latest discover when they were called to order by Boy.

"Sailormans come. Meet Chief Shit Head."

They followed cautiously as Boy lead them to the communal hootch. When they approached they noticed most of the surrounding natives were just lying about and seemed to be a bit lethargic. Two of them were sprawled comfortably near the hootch pounding on drums for no apparent reason, not in the rhythmic manner that might be expected but just banging for the hell of it. None of the natives seemed to be the least bit excited about the arrival of Boy and the group of strange foreigners.

As they approached, a native man exited the hootch with a large gourd that he dipped into an even larger pot of liquid. When doing so he spied the arriving foreigners, grew a little bug eyed and quickly darted back inside yelling something unintelligible. The shore party paused and from within they heard an equally unintelligible deep blustering voice respond, after which the surrounding natives began to stir and rise, eying the strangers curiously. The drumming ceased and all became quiet. Finally, after a long moment, the tall bull of a man who was Chief Shit Head emerged from the hootch. He was large, muscular, with a bit of a potbelly but all in all quite impressive with colorful regalia, hastily applied face paint, a lethal looking spear, and a quickly donned headdress; which seemed to sit a bit askew though it was difficult to tell being his head rolled like a ship in the water with each breath. He paused regally, observing the group overall then moved forward to the Crimson Glory company and inspected them more closely. He paused again and stepped back, noticing their war torn baboon blood covered appearance and developed a more serious demeanor. He looked down to Boy.

"Bad Coons?"

Boy nodded confirmation then the Chief moved closer to inspect his visitors individually. He first approached Jonesy and observed his small being with curiosity from top to bottom then moved on to Bobbie and stopped. He touched her hair, squeezed her arms and leaned in to glance down her shirt. He looked to boy, unimpressed, thinking her too damn skinny. Boy simply shrugged his shoulders. From Bobbie the Chief turned to find himself face to face with Bart who offered up his ever pleasing but currently nervous signature shit-eating smile. The Chief automatically returned the smile exposing a mouth full of large white teeth. He touched Bart's blond hair, squeezed his arm, then as an afterthought, leaned to look down his shirt. The Chief's smile grew larger and Bart's smile began to dissipate as he slowly backed away.

Then Chief Shit Head stepped back, suddenly threw his arms up thrusting his spear into the air and shouted with great volume and authority, "BOLU!"

Like some crazed tent revival preacher high on his own Jesus lightning, the Chief's eyes rolled back, rigor mortis set in and not unlike a downed towering California redwood, he fell long and straight and flat on his face. The group looked upon the now defunct hulking royal figure with surprised curiosity. Boy looked down and shook his head in disgust.

"What the hell happened?" asked Bart.

"He gots Sailorman Shit Head sickness," answered Boy.

"What?" asked Jonesy.

"They all gots crazy Sailorman Shit Head sickness."

"Sickness," asked Bart. "Is that contagious?"

"Sailorman Shit Head teach them make bolu. When they drink bolu they catch Sailorman Shit Head sickness," explained Boy. "Sometimes whole village catch. Sometimes catch for long time. Sometimes make everybody mean like bad coons. Sometimes make everybody dance naked."

"Bolu?" said Captain Buckmaster.

Bobbie kneeled down and inspected the fallen Chief then offered a surprising prognosis.

"This bloke's drunk as a bloomin' dingo!"

By the time evening fell the shore party had merged easily in among the natives and was now spread about the village. Irish was in discussion with a few of the bolu brew masters at the big pot and various others of the expedition casually relaxed, were cleaning their weapons or sleeping. Big Tiny sat near a fire and tossed the rugby ball back and forth with Boy while Stanley, the Captain, Bobbie, Jonesy and Bart were sitting and conversing around another small fire near the open ocean side of the volcanic basin. Earlier, two of the natives escorted one of the ship's crew along a safe route back to the beach with orders to return the launches to the ship and bring the ship around to this side of the island. From where they sat a near full moon now offered a comforting view of the Crimson Glory at anchor.

"Now let me get this straight," Stanley addressed Jonesy. "A long time ago these people used to live out there in that ancient city."

"Correct," answered Jonesy. "It took a while for me to decipher their language. It's kind of a mix of Aborigine, Farsi and a plethora of African and Pacific dialects. An Indonesian potluck of words, you might say. I'm still not sure I've got it right. Guess we're better off sticking with that Sailorman Shit Head English of theirs."

"A plethorwhat?" asked Bart.

"It means, a whole lot, Bart. Like a bunch of bananas," continued Jonesy. "Hey, I thought you were a genius scholarship student at Princeton."

"I am. Doesn't mean I speak foreign languages with words like plethora though."

Jonesy just looked at Bart and shook his head then continued, "Now as I was saying, the way I understand it, they're the descendants of the original occupants of the city who were driven to live here many centuries ago when they lost a war with the god of the fire mountain named Myuko."

"Yeah, those gods will get ya every time," observed

Bart.

"Myuko?" came the Captain.

"Yes. It's kind of a love story, actually."

"Love story," said Bobbie. "You gotta be kidding, right mate?"

"Not at all. They say Myuko was put here to protect them from all the demons of the island; which is why they built that great wall, to keep out the demons. But, and this is the love story part, this Myuko became angered because this young prince prevented the people's annual virgin sacrifice. Apparently the virgin in question was the prince's bride to be and he didn't want to give up a good thing."

"Sacrifice?" asked Stanley.

"Yes, to Myuko. You know, like the Hawaiians did with their volcano god, Pele."

"The Hawaiians sacrificed virgins?" asked Bart.

"I think so. Saw it in a movie once," answered Jonesy. "Anyway, this Myuko destroyed the city, chased off the people and left his devil army, the baboons, to prevent them from ever returning."

"It's like one of those old bizarre biblical tales," said Bobbie. "Virgin sacrifices to some boogie man. Sounds like they've all got a few kangaroos loose in the top paddock if you ask me."

"Wow, can you imagine that?" said Bart.

"Destroying that great city? I'm afraid it wouldn't be a very pretty sight to imagine," said Captain Buckmaster.

"No. I mean sacrificing a perfectly good virgin,"

returned Bart.

"I don't understand," came Stanley. "Whoever built that city weren't a primitive people like these. How do you account for their regression?"

"I'm not sure but they said after the people were driven from the city they split and became many tribes. Some here on the island and some went to the sea, which I suppose means they all went their separate ways and took their knowledge and secrets with them."

"So just the light headed blokes stayed home on the farm, eh Jonesy?" speculated Bobbie.

"Either that or too damn much bolu," Jonesy laughed.

Just then Irish joined the group, carrying a gourd full of bolu. He sat comfortably and took a generous swig then offered the same to the others.

"Anybody wanna' dance naked?"

They all declined.

"It's that native bolu. I'll be admittin' it ain't fine Irish whiskey and it's a bit fruity but it'll certainly warm yer willie on a cold night in Killarney."

"That stuff will make you stupid," declared Bart.

"Best go easy on that concoction, Irish. We're heading into the bush in the morning," advised the Captain.

"Aye Capt'n," replied Irish, taking a final taste then tossing the remaining bolu into the fire where it exploded into high flames. The flare up caused Irish to fall off his seat. He looked to the gourd, "A bit temperamental I'd say."

Bart was still brewing about Jonesy's story and moved to his side to further explore the subject, "Now, this was hundreds of years ago. Right?" he asked Jonesy.

Jonesy nodded a yes.

"So this Myuko god guy, he's probably long dead, right. Or flew the coup or something, right?"

"Guess so," speculated Jonesy.

"Guess so?"

"Hey, give me a break. I'm a cook not a damn mystic," declared Jonesy as he rose and left the circle to retire for the night.

"Guess so?" Bart repeated to himself. "Guess so?"

chapter 13

It was hot, damn hot as the ivy league expeditionary troop trudged along in single file, loaded down with equipment and weapons. Stanley led the way, hacking through the brush with a machete. He was followed by Bart, Captain Buckmaster, the thirteen Princeton rugby boys, Jonesy, Bobbie, and three of the crew of the Crimson Glory. What they had seen of the jungle on this island so far was everything an uncorrupted jungle should be, dense and full of wild sounds, twisted trees, vines, broad leafed overgrowth and critters of all kinds, except in this jungle everything was abnormally bigger, much bigger.

The tired sweaty column halted with a signal from Stanley and everyone relaxed to take a breather. About that time there came a rustle in the bush behind them causing each to quickly bring their weapons to bear. After the experience in the ancient city they had all become slightly trigger-happy.

"What's that? Baboons?" said a wide-eyed Edward.

They looked about, guns at the ready, then another rustle and Edward was about to fire blindly when Bobbie stopped him.

"Wait!" she said, reaching out and redirecting his rifle skyward.

She looked intensely into the bush, moved in closer, paused, then disappeared into the jungle altogether. When she finally reappeared she had Boy in tow by the ear.

"It's just a little ankle biter," she said with a smile.

"Boy, I told you to stay home," scolded Stanley. "It's too dangerous for you here."

"Not more dangerous than Chief Father Shit Head. He drink more bolu again. Make him mean. Give Boy ass kick."

"We can't send him back alone," said Bobbie. "It's too far."

About that time up walked Big Tiny looking down on the boy like some coach who was dissatisfied with his little Pop Warner phenom.

Boy stood at his feet looking way up to lock eyes then offered a crooked little half-ass smile.

"I got 'em," said Big Tiny, who reached down and offered the boy a hand. Boy took it and was swiftly lifted up to land on Big Tiny's shoulders like an organ grinder's monkey.

"Wow, you mighty big bastard. Like Myuko," boy observed as he sat tall in the saddle.

The boy's statement alarmed Bart who quickly deduced it must be the result of first hand knowledge. He turned to Jonesy, "Guess so?"

Jonesy just shrugged in return.

By mid day the group found themselves still hacking their way through the jungle, occasionally being spooked by strange creatures and birds as the creatures themselves were spooked and panicked by the human intrusion into their wild world. They eventually came upon a broad shallow river, paused, sized it up then stripped off their gear and began to cross. Holding the gear above their heads, most navigated the crossing safely but with some difficulty. Short little Jonesy however had an exceptionally difficult time with the height of the river reaching up to his shoulders. He could hardly keep his pack above his head as he struggled then eventually succumbed and went under but was quickly retrieved by the back of his shirt by Big Tiny. Big Tiny easily hauled him through the water with one hand all the way to the bank of the river all the while continuing to carry boy on his shoulders. The last of them reached the other side where Bart stood taking a drink from his canteen. Looking back to the river where they had just crossed he caught a glimpse of something in the water.

He then saw it again, something very large, maybe thirty feet long and crocodile like as it surfaced then dove. He stared a moment then quickly turned to the others.

"Did you see that? Hey, did... did you see that?"

They paid him little mind as they packed up and moved on. He followed; constantly looking over his shoulder then tapped Stewart.

"Stewart, did you see that?"

Stewart shrugged a no, slung his pack and moved on.

"You didn't... It was... How could you guys miss that thing? Shit, it was big and... Hey, hey..." Bart continued while walking backward until the river was out of sight and he felt safe.

Near the end of the day, still trudging through the jungle with Stanley and Henry leading, they broke through to find themselves in a clearing of low grass.

"Gonna' be dark soon," observed Henry.

"Yeah," agreed Stanley who turned to the rest of the company as they emerged into the clearing. "Getting dark. We better set up here for the night."

Bart and the Captain joined him as he pulled the old sailor's map and a compass from his pocket. He looked up to the smoldering volcano in the far distance for reference then to his compass.

"I make it about a day if the terrain isn't too bad," he said pointing to the volcano. "East side base of that big volcano according to the map."

Big Tiny walked by, reached up and easily lifted Boy

off his shoulders and tossed him to the ground.

"There you go champ."

The others spread out and started dumping their packs and flopping to the ground, more than grateful for the much needed respite.

By nightfall they had all settled in around a few small fires, some sleeping, some talking, two were walking with weapons slung while two others stood a casual guard near the perimeter of the clearing. Big Tiny was asleep, snoring like a jackhammer. Next to him laid Boy who couldn't sleep because of the jackhammer. He reached over and flicked Big Tiny's nose. The snoring stopped and the boy rolled over. Big Tiny, his eyes still closed, smiled.

Nearby lay a weary Bart whose eyes were also shut as he tried fruitlessly to sleep. From the surrounding jungle and hills came a full variety of eerie sounds of varied nocturnal animals interspersed with the more pronounced unfamiliar sounds of things reptilian and seemingly very large. Bart's eyes opened and he stared up to the stars.

The following day as the sun rose over the island, like most everywhere else in the world, all things stretched and came alive with anticipation. All except Bart Haile who was the only member of the company still asleep, having finally managed to fall asleep from sheer exhaustion in the wee dark hours of pre dawn. Bart's rest and dreams were rudely interrupted however by a boot in the butt causing him to stir, roll over and force open his eyes to discover standing above him a smiling Stanley Wellington.

"Still with me, old man?" smiled Stanley as he lowered a cup of coffee.

Bart wasn't quite ready to speak feeling it was just too damn early so he shook his head yes, accepted the coffee and sat up slowly. The aroma of the coffee and a small sampling sip seemed to finally release his vocal cords.

"Tell me I'm still dreaming. Please tell me I'm dreaming this entire expedition."

"No dream, old man. We're right where you want us to be."

"I want. What's this I want stuff? You're the one who... and... and I can't say I'm overly impressed by your choice of hotels either," he grumbled then sipped the coffee again. "The neighbors are noisy as hell and the beds are lumpier than shit."

Stanley laughed then nodded to the edge of the clearing and the nearby jungle, "Facilities are over there."

"Oh, right," acknowledged Bart.

He rose drudgingly with all the grace of an old geriatric mule with one hoof in the grave and with his coffee in hand, stumbled to the edge of the clearing where he opened the fly on his trousers and looked around to see Bobbie. She offered a pleasant morning smile. Embarrassed, he moved further into the jungle behind a large tree then dug into his trousers with one hand and held and sipped his coffee with the other. His eyes were closed with the pleasant relief of his morning piss until he came to hear the deep-throated sound of disapproval, the kind of sound you might hear from a very large unfriendly dog who doesn't want company. Except bigger, much much bigger. Bart opened his eyes to realize he was now pissing on someone's foot, a very, very large hairy foot, much larger than Bart himself and then some. He looked up and up and up to discover standing there looking down at him was a gorilla. A big damn gorilla. A big like Kong damn gorilla and it flashed through Bart's mind that was he not already pissing he would be pissing in his pants. He initially froze in fear then dropped the coffee, threw out his arms and let out a scream greater than any sound he had ever made in his entire life.

"Ahhhhhhhhhhh!"

Then - are you ready for this - the gorilla did the same, throwing up its arms and screaming, except with a decibel range that would shatter the fillings in your teeth.

Bart panicked, turned and ran.

Then - are you ready for this - the gorilla did the same, turned and ran into the jungle, except in doing so it happened to knock down every damn tree in its path. Crash! Bam! Boom!

Bart ran to the center of the clearing where everyone stood looking at the gorilla's tornado like path of destruction through the jungle. Then Bart stopped, frozen, looking up in the opposite direction as everyone else and he screamed again, louder, longer, except no one could hear his scream because it was drowned out by the horrendous shrieking spine gripping roar of a dinosaur. A big dinosaur. One of those big nasty ferocious meatasaurus kind of dinosaurs and it had just dropped in for breakfast.

Everyone in the expedition quickly turned to discover their uninvited breakfast guest then scrambled in a panic to gather their weapons.

"Holy SHIT!" exclaimed Jonesy. In Chinese.

His comment was quickly repeated in English by most everyone in the group except Bart who could find no words at all.

Shots rang out from all around the camp with everyone shooting everything they had at the huge intruder and achieving nothing other than just pissing it off big time. The creature screamed, roared and showed more huge deadly teeth than a piano had keys.

"Tiny! Get the bazooka!" yelled Stanley.

Big Tiny ran and retrieved his bazooka and was quickly joined by Irish with the weapon's ammo. He then dropped to one knee and shouldered the stove pipe weapon as Irish loaded a round into the back. Irish tapped a ready signal on Big Tiny's shoulder and just as he was about to pull the trigger the frightening meatasaurus gave off a particularly threatening roaring scream directed right at him as if to say, *Don't even think about it.*

Okay, so Big Tiny was a little intimidated and he flinched and fired and... missed, blowing up a perfectly innocent tree. Meanwhile, everyone was still shooting everything and getting nowhere. The creature, momentarily distracted by the blast of the bazooka round, turned back ready to charge.

Irish began to reload but had trouble getting the ammo into the back of the bouncing bazooka.

"Hold the damn thing still, boyo!"

"It's not me!" yelled Big Tiny.

Then both men realized the ground was trembling like an earthquake, trembling because from the jungle behind them, like an all-American linebacker on a good day, charged the big gorilla; which roared, dove and tackled the uninvited dinosaur. The gunfire ceased but the real war had just begun with the two giants in conflict in a tangled mass of violent screaming and shrieking, knocking down trees, rolling through anything and everything that got in the way including people who scattered in all directions. It was a fearsome sight of which few words are adequate for description and certainly none to capture the emotions of the observers with the exception of little Jonesy as he desperately ran for safety.

"HOLY SHIT! HOLY SHIT!" he continued to yell. In Chinese.

Finally the gorilla broke free, rose and threw a right cross that would take out the Brooklyn Bridge. The deadly meatasaurus went down with a huge thud and the

angry gorilla dove in for more. Slam! Bam! Knocking all
the cool out of the beast and breaking nearly every bone
from navel to nose. The beast lay there squealing and
groaning as the gorilla came away cautiously. It
squirmed and squealed once again and the gorilla levied
a final sledge hammer whack on its head. End of match.
New champion, gorilla!

The Crimson Glory troop lay spread about on the
ground, staring in disbelief, confused and wondering if
they would be next. The huge gorilla looked to its dead
opponent and no, it didn't stand and pound its chest in
victory but instead sat, exhausted, looked to the members
of the expedition, smiled, lifted its hands and just
shrugged, leading all to conclude that something wasn't
quite right with this particular ape. Everyone continued
to stare and the gorilla continued to smile. Bart rubbed
his forehead, discovered a trickle of blood and passed
out.

Bart was still laying on the ground being nursed by
Bobbie when he regained consciousness a few minutes
later, looked up and saw the gorilla sitting and staring
down at him. He immediately jumped but was restrained
by Bobbie.

"No, no. it's alright."

Bart looked at her as though she were crazy then
again at the gorilla. The gorilla smiled.

"I don't think it will hurt us," said Bobbie.

Jonesy approached with a canteen of water and

offered it to Bart who looked at him and was about to
repeat the *guess so* when he was cut off.

"Don't say it," said Jonesy.

They were joined by Stanley who easily picked up on
Bart's concern about the gorilla.

"Well, I guess introductions are in order here,"
smiled Stanley. "Bart, meet Monkey. Monkey, this is
Bart."

Bart looked at Stanley then the gorilla then stared at
everyone as though they'd just been released from a
funny farm. He then heard the sporting sounds of people
having fun and turned to see a rugby game in progress.
Boy had the ball and Big Tiny, chewing his cigar, had
Boy as they plowed through the rest of the players, all
laughing and acting as though just beyond the game there
didn't lay the biggest and only dead meatasaurus they
had ever seen. The gorilla's attention was drawn to the
sounds of the game. It rose, went and sat on the dead
dino and watched with interest.

"I saw the movie. It's not supposed to be like this,"
said Bart.

"And just what movie would that be, mate?" asked a
bewildered Bobbie.

chapter 14

The expedition recovered and regrouped from the frightening experience of their rude awakening and got underway once again. The jungle seemed to be getting more primitive and difficult as they moved further inland, slowing their progress toward their destination. They continued with high spirits however and with a most unlikely escort in the form of a tag along near thirty-foot tall gorilla.

Bart transferred his rifle to his other hand and adjusted his pack while giving an occasional glance over his shoulder to Monkey who was following close behind. Monkey smiled.

"Boy. Monkey. Take me to your leader. You know Stanley's got a serious lack of imagination," Bart complained to anyone who would listen. "Monkey. What kind of name is Monkey? And who designated him the name maker anyway. I'm sure glad he wasn't around when I was born. Probably would have named me *meat* or *goo* or something like that."

"I think he likes you," said Jonesy.

"What?"

"Monkey. I think he likes you."

"She," corrected Bobbie.

"What?" asked Jonesy.

"She. It's a she."

"Are you sure," asked Bart.

Bobbie turned and looked at Bart and Jonesy with a knowing raised eyebrow.

"Oh. Right," Bart conceded. He thought a moment then questioned Jonesy, "Hey, wait a minute. If it's a girl then what was all that horse manure about virgin sacrifices?"

"Hey, I don't know," answered Jonesy. "I'm just a cook, remember? Maybe she's... Well, you know..."

"You mean..."

Bart looked back at Monkey then back to Jonesy. Jonesy shrugged. He looked again at Monkey and again she smiled.

"No. I don't believe it. Not gorillas."

Entering into a forest of exceptionally large trees and being taken by the impressive spectacle of their imposing height, most of the party failed to notice the obstacle of an expansive split in the earth until they had almost reached its edge. It was easily over a thousand feet deep and much too wide to throw a rope or create some form of makeshift solution.

"Well now, that's certainly an impressive fork in the road, eh lads," observed Irish as he leaned over carefully to inspect the massive gorge.

"There's no way across that thing," offered Mule. "It's too wide."

"I'm afraid you might be right," agreed Stanley. "Not even any trees close enough on this side that we could fell and use as a bridge."

"The size of these trees. Are you kidding?" injected Chrisfield. "It would take days to cut one down even with axes and all we have are machetes."

"Guess we'll have to skirt the edge of this thing until we can find a way across," said Stanley. "Looks like it goes on for miles. We could loose maybe an entire day."

They stood there, small among the giant trees and helpless to cross the wide chasm when the ground suddenly began to tremble. Then came a roar and they turned just in time to see Monkey rush past and launch herself across the broad gap. She landed on the other side with a boom just barely clearing the edge, looked down into the gorge, offered a sigh of relief then turned and inspected a nearby tree. Satisfied it was adequate, she lowered her shoulder and gave it a hardy shove. The tree swayed then began to fall then stopped. Monkey looked at it, grunted, slapped it, then shoved and heaved again until its roots tore from the ground and it began to fall across the gorge. Monkey's actions were a feat of genius for your average oversized ape thought the group until they realized the enormous tree was coming down directly on top of them and forcing them to scatter desperately in all directions. The tree landed with a tremendous crash causing birds and beast throughout the forest to rise in a concert of screaming disturbance. Monkey had created a bridge, albeit not to neatly. She smiled an embarrassed apology for the misdirection then shook her hand, bidding them to pass over.

"Way to go, girl! Good on ya," yelled Bobbie as she began climbing through the branches, onto the long wide trunk and across to the other side.

They rest followed in single file, careful not to look down and let the extreme distance to the bottom of the gorge intimidate them. The boy however couldn't resist a glance into the depths of the gorge below, leaned a little too far and began to fall when he was quickly snatched back then picked up and carried by Big Tiny. Bart was last in line and was moving across slowly and carefully. When he was midway across, the tree jerked and rolled. Bart lost his balance and fell, losing his rifle but somehow holding on to the tree's thick bark for dear life. He watched as the rifle fell endlessly to the bottom of the gorge then looked up to see the others jumping off the tree bridge at the far end. Looking back he was surprised to discover a large lizard had decided to join in their crossing. The creature was so large that the tree rolled from its excessive weight and size. Large enough, Bart quickly surmised, to swallow him whole.

He rose carefully and ran for the other side but fell again when the tree jolted and rolled to the left. The giant reptile was now nearing the middle of the impromptu bridge, hissing, threatening, its tongue darting out for a taste of Bart's ass. The others, having reached safety, now had their weapons up and were firing repeatedly, only to realize their bullets were as useless against the thick natural armor of this creature as they had been against the dinosaur earlier that same day. Bart rose again and took a few desperate steps when the creature bolted to catch him, causing the tree to bounce and roll radically, throwing him off the tree altogether. The fear of the thousand-foot fall seized his entire being but just as he fell he was snatched out of the air by Monkey who brought him in to safety, set him down and smiled. She then looked to the big lizard, grew seriously pissed off, let out a roar of anger and grabbing the root ball of the tree, wrestled it over the side. The huge tree along with the lizard tumbled down the thousand feet and when it crashed to the bottom a spine-chilling screech of pain echoed off the walls of the gorge announcing the reptile's death.

Bart looked up to monkey with relief and a smile of gratitude. Monkey offered a girlish grin in return and nudged Bart affectionately with a single finger unintentionally knocking him flat on his ass. Surprised, she offered a simple gorilla equivalent of an *oops*. Bart stared a moment then laughed. Boy began laughing uncontrollably and was soon joined by the others who laughed as much from relief from danger as from Bart's situation. Monkey caught on and joined in with a few chuckles of her own. When Bart came to his feet Monkey knocked him down again and roared with laughter. Monkey had discovered more than a few new friends, she had also discovered a new game.

Bart simply laid there, the ass end of a very, very big joke, but happy to be alive.

chapter 15

With the expedition moving further inland the forest of giant trees and jungle became less dense and demanding. When they came to a sparse high rise of ground they could see out over their final challenge which had to be traversed in order to reach their destination at the base of the great smoking mountain. The view was magnificent, showing miles and miles of lush growth, hills and valleys, and two enormous high misty waterfalls which eventually merged into a single river that weaved its way to the coast. Situated in the midst of it all was their destination volcano.

"We can cross there above the falls," said Stanley,

pointing out over the expansive island.

"Look at that will ya. It's paradise," admired Chrisfield.

"It's dangerous," a practical Captain Buckmaster reminded the young man.

"Aye, that it is Skipper," agreed Irish. "Like a beautiful succubus with designs on your soul and your life's blood."

"Now those aren't the words of a fine romantic Irish poet adventurer," said Bobbie, looking out over the island.

"Oh yes, mum. They're not only the words of a fine Irish romantic poet adventurer," he agreed readily. "They're also the words of an Irishman thrice married and as many times forlorned. Now wouldn't that call for a romantic venturesome soul?"

Bobbie looked to Irish with reservations, "Three times?"

"Perhaps they had a bit of just cause," he admitted. "But not so much as to dull a man's soul, I would think."

"You're a marvel of a man, Irish," smiled Bobbie, giving him a peck on the cheek.

Irish grew a broad smile and blushed.

"And you're full of shit," she added as she moved off to join the men who had started down the hill.

Irish's smile quickly turned to disappointment until Bart came up and patted him on the back.

"Don't let it bother you, *me boyo*," offered Bart with a laugh. "Happens to me all the time."

"Is that suppose to be reassuring?" ask Irish.

Half a day later the expedition had worked its way around the falls and was nearing their destination at the foot of the volcano. Hiking through a rolling area littered with large boulders, stone formations and less growth, Bart was again bringing up the rear of the column. This was primarily because Monkey had now appointed herself Bart's protector, closely following him everywhere and making his position anywhere else in the column too cumbersome and dangerous for the others. And then there was the matter of hygiene. Monkey may have been a lady but she smelled more like the east end of a dead camel heading west.

A few of the rugby boys insisted Monkey was sweet as a flower and that Bart was the guilty pungent party but conceded they had become so attached that it was difficult to distinguish between the two. Aromatically that is. In spite of the scent of the situation, Bart now had himself a near thirty-foot tall loyal lap dog with an unending sense of humor demonstrated by the constant desire to play the ups and downs game. About every ten minutes Monkey would reach out and tap Bart on the ass knocking him to the ground. She would then chuckle and back away only to work her way closer again as they walked along. As she once again tapped Bart on the ass nearly knocking him to the ground he finally turned to set out a few rules regarding their relationship.

"Okay, listen up," Bart scolded Monkey. "If we're going to be friends you've got to learn some manners.

First of all…"

Bart was suddenly interrupted by excited chatter and activity from up ahead of the column. He turned and ran to catch up and as he rounded a large hill of boulders he found everyone looking up to the side of the volcanic mountain where there sat high and dry, overgrown with vines and vegetation, a large four-masted ship. The huge carcass of a sea vessel sat smashed against the mountain, her hull breached and masts and rigging crushed.

"This isn't possible," observed Captain Buckmaster. "Even the biggest storm or tsunami wouldn't carry a ship this far inland. It's just not possible."

"I'd say just about anything's possible on this island, Skipper," said Irish.

Stanley walked the length of the long ship's hull until he reached the transom and looked up. He was joined by Bart.

"My God, it's the Saint Jane," said Stanley.

The lettering was old but still visible and clearly spelled out, *Saint Jane - San Francisco*. Stanley and Bart looked to each other with a similar thought then turned and looked to Monkey. Monkey shrugged her shoulders as if to say, *Don't look at me, I didn't do it.*

Big Tiny lowered Boy to the ground and looked up to the ship, not noticing when the boy wondered off.

Stanley perched himself on a rock, whipped out the map and studied it. Moments later he started pointing repeatedly at the X on the old parchment map and announced, "Hey, this is it. This is it!"

He stood, excited and pointed to the ship. Bart cringed; sure Stanley was going to dust off another old cliché about X's marking the spot.

"The... The Saint Jane marks the Spot!" declared Stanley.

Bart looked to Stanley, relieved.

"What?" asked Stanley.

"For a second there I thought you were going to say, X marks the spot."

"Well it does."

Bart rolled his eyes upward, "We really have to work on that imagination of yours."

"Hey, this was all your idea, remember?" said Stanley with a smile.

"My idea!"

He slapped Bart on the back and turned to address the rest of the group, "Spread out. Look for signs of digging. A mining tunnel or a cave."

"My idea. What the hell do you mean, my idea?" defended Bart. "It wasn't my idea. I was perfectly happy at Princeton being an almost lawyer."

Boy's voice rang out drawing everyone's attention to the deck of the derelict ship.

"Sailorman Tiny! Sailorman Tiny, come see!"

Big Tiny looked up to discover Boy leaning precariously over the ship's rail.

"I find. I find Sailorman Shit Head's big hole!"

"We've got to improve that boy's language skills," observed Jonesy.

"Boy, get down from there! It's not safe!" called Big Tiny.

The boy climbed over and down the side of the ship with the aid of some old downed rigging and vines then ran to Big Tiny.

"Big hole in big boat. Same as big hole in mountain."

"You mean a big hole that goes *into* the side of mountain?" asked Stanley as he joined them.

"Yes. Sailorman Shit Head's big hole where he dig rocks," answered Boy. "Why Shit Head want to dig rocks anyway? He drink too much bolu?"

"Yeah, kid," laughed Stanley. "Something like that."

Stanley tossed his gear and he and a few others were starting up the side of the ship when they were cautioned by Captain Buckmaster.

"Hold on there, gentlemen. I don't know much about mining but I know a perilous ship when I see one. We best be careful. She's rotted and her back's broken. She could come off that mountain easy when we start poking around in there."

Just then Bart got a little nudge from the playful Monkey that inspired a possible solution.

"Wait a minute. I've got an idea." Bart looked to Monkey, trying his best to sign his directions with his hands as he spoke, "Monkey, move the boat. Push. Like the tree. Push."

Monkey looked down, reached over, nudged Bart and knocked him on his ass. Then let loose a grunt and chuckle.

"No no," said Bart from his place on the ground. "Not me." He rose and pointed to the ship. "The ship. Push the ship. Like this. Monkey move the ship."

Bart went to the Saint Jane, grabbed a line of rigging and pretended to pull it over. Monkey got the idea and went to the ship, reached out over the deck with one hand and pulled. The ship rocked, tearing at the decades of growth and vines.

"That's it," yelled Bart. "Pull! Pull the big boat down!"

Monkey reached out with both hands and yanked on the Saint Jane until it began to break away with the sound of cracking, ripping timbers. Then the huge ship began to roll. Monkey, Bart and the others quickly moved away as the old vessel literally broke in two at the center, the forward half sliding and rolling violently down the hill to finally crash into a large formation of rocks. When the dust cleared they looked up to discover in the side of the mountain behind the remaining half of the ship was a large cave entrance. A few cheers went up for Monkey and the discovery of Sailorman Shit Head's hole but just as they began to climb up to the newly exposed entrance the ground rumbled and a landslide of earth and boulders came down the side of the mountain, sending them scurrying out of the way and burying the ship and the cave entrance altogether.

The hearts and emotions of the entire expedition crew sank.

"This fuckin' island's starting to piss me off," said

little Jonesy, in Italian.

"What, no Chinese?" asked Bobbie.

"No. That one just felt better in Italian," he answered.

"Well, that's just great," said Chrisfield. "Now what are we going to do?"

Bobbie stepped up, studied the massive mound of rubble, dropped her pack and turned back to the group.

"I got this," she said with confidence. "Irish, get the dynamite."

An hour later Irish and Bobbie were running a fuse back from the pile of rocks and debris blocking the cave entrance. Bobbie cut the line and handed the roll of remaining fuse to Irish.

"Match," she demanded.

Irish handed her a match. She took it, stuck the match on her ass and lit the fuse then casually walked to the safety of the large rock formation where lay the front half carcass of the Saint Jane. They all stood about watching the burning fuse until Irish took off running then realizing the wisdom therein, everyone else quickly followed.

As Bart ran for cover he looked back to see Monkey was still squatting and curiously observing the fuse with intense interest. Bart stopped.

"Monkey! Monkey run!," he called

Monkey looked to Bart but didn't' move.

"Run! Monkey run!" he repeated.

The fuse burned swiftly, getting ever closer to the large bundle of dynamite buried beneath the rubble. They all began desperately calling for Monkey to run. She looked up then back to the fuse and reached out to touch it.

"No Monkey, no!" called Bart. "Monkey come!"

Monkey finally meandered over and joined them, not understanding any of their ridiculous actions. Bart looked to the fuse and seeing it was about to reach the dynamite, jumped behind the rocks, crouched over and covered his head. Thinking she was learning a new game, Monkey chuckled and crouched behind the rocks just as she had seen Bart do. Monkey however, was just too damn big and so was her ass which stuck far out beyond the sheltering rock formation.

The fuse burned through the final inches reaching Bobbie's buried stash of explosive. The subsequent explosion was tremendously loud and massive, leaving everyone to quickly surmise she had used far too much dynamite. The blocked cave, a good part of the mountainside and the buried half of the Saint Jane blew sky high and wide with debris rocketing over and around in every direction, continuing to fall for what seemed an eternity. When all grew silent everyone slowly rose from their safe positions and peeked out to discover a huge hole in the side of the mountain. Stanley looked over to Bobbie and Irish who offered a sheepish smile.

"Well, I guess you really can blow shit up," said an impressed Stanley.

"She ain't just pretty, Gov, she can scramble a few eggs as well," laughed Irish.

Stanley and Bobbie exchanged an affectionate smile that didn't go unnoticed by Irish.

"Guess dynamite does that to people, eh?" he observed.

Monkey was wide eyed and seriously disturbed by the explosion. She stood and looked at all the damage then she scrunched her face, opened her mouth and whined as she moved her hands to her backside. She moaned again and looked around to her ass to discover a large splinter of wood from the Saint Jane sticking out of her left butt cheek.

"Oh shit!" exclaimed Bart when he spied her injury. "Oh, that's got to hurt."

"Wow!" exclaimed Boy. "Sailorman Shit Head's hole is much big now."

"Kid, they would really love you at Oxford," observed Jonesy.

chapter 16

Monkey lie stretched out flat on her belly with a small tree between her teeth while perched and kneeling on top of her ass were Bart, Jonesy and Bobbie preparing to perform surgery. The situation was obviously no fun for the big hairy girl and the discomfort was evident by her many facial contortions. Bobbie's probing with a sharp knife shot bolts of pain through Monkey's butt causing her to grind down harder on the tree. Bart cold hear it crack as she bit down, bringing him to enter into one of his nervous ramblings as he often did in times of stress and at the sight of blood. Bobbie and Jonesy however remained focused on the dirty work.

"I don't believe this. It's just too unbelievable. Killer baboons, alcoholic natives, dinosaurs, and now I'm sitting on a stinkin' monkey's ass doing surgery. I'm supposed to be a lawyer not an ass doctor."

Jonesy and Bobbie offered a simultaneous response, "Shut up."

"Here it comes," announced Bobbie as she pulled the large piece of wood from Monkey's butt cheek. "It's coming. Here it… I'm getting it."

Monkey dug an eight foot hole in the earth with each hand as she painfully cringed and gripped the ground then bit the tree between her teeth clean through.

"There, I've got it!" announced Bobbie.

Bobbie sat up, a bloody knife in one hand and a six foot long bloody splinter of wood in the other. She handed the wood to Bart who looked away in disgust and tossed it aside. When he looked back, Jonesy was pouring the contents of a full canteen on the bloody wound.

"What's that?" asked Bart.

"Irish's bolu," answered Jonesy. "Best thing I could find to disinfect a big hairy ass."

Bobbie lifted a ten inch long makeshift needle attached to some thin line she retrieved from the Saint Jane intended to use for suturing.

"Alright, lets close her up, mate."

Bart squinted and leaned away at the sight as they attacked the task with sincere intensity, concluding the job in a matter of minutes.

"There you go, Bart. She'll be apples in no time," smiled Bobbie.

But Doctor Bobbie's reassuring words went unheard for Bart now lay passed out atop the big monkey's ass.

Monkey smiled a sigh of relief.

Following a brief examination of the open end of the cave Stanley and the others determined they would explore further in the morning. They were tired and had been through enough that day already and weren't eager to take off excitedly into the dark unknown regions of a tentatively hazardous volcano. Their current priority was to establish and secure camp and plan and sort out the needed equipment for the next day's exploration.

With the coming of evening the duly exhausted members of the expedition spent their time eating, resting and some were already sleeping. Bart, Jonesy and a few of the rugby boys sat by one of the two small fires chatting about the many missed comforts of home. Monkey sat nearby, fascinated by the fire and occasionally reached over to touch the flames with her finger.

"Hey, stop that," Bart told Monkey. "You're going to burn yourself. Then you'll have a bandage on your ass and your finger. Everybody will think you're a dunce or something."

"You think she knows what you're saying there, Bart?" asked Kicker.

"You know Bart, it's kind of interesting how people, or in this case, a person and a gorilla, come to be attracted to each other," observed Jonesy.

"Yeah," added one of the gang. "I guess you might even say it's some kind of an animal attraction," added Kicker.

They all laughed.

"I'll go along with that," said another. "But which one's the animal?"

"Take it easy fellahs," laughed Bart. "You might insult this lady, and judging from what we've seen so far I think it's obvious we don't want to piss her off. Isn't that right, Monkey?"

Monkey chuckled and gave Bart a light tap on the head.

"Roast beef, potatoes and gravy, muffins full of Cape Cod cranberries drowned in butter. And that custard my mother makes. You fellahs haven't lived until you've had my mother's custard," said Mule.

"I'll tell you what," Bart offered to Mule. "If we find those diamonds I'll buy you a ship load of those cranberries and you can eat muffins till the cows come home."

"Only a ship load?" asked Mule.

"Well, we've got to leave room for all that custard," laughed Bart.

"Hey, I can cook you boys that kind of stuff," said Jonesy.

"Sure you can," said Stinky. "The question is could we eat it after you do."

There was hardy laughter all around.

An insulted Jonesy rose to leave the circle and

responded in a deceptively congenial manner, in Chinese, "May your rice bowl always be full and your chopsticks always be stuck up your asses."

Stanley, Bobbie and Irish sat in quiet conversation near the other campfire.

"You're one of them, aren't you?" Bobbie asked of Stanley.

Stanley and Irish, confused, both looked to Bobbie.

"One of them?" asked Stanley.

"One of those tight lipped fellahs who won't let anybody in," she clarified. "Got a lot of those where I come from."

"And why do you suppose that is, mum?" asked Irish.

"Well, some say it's because they're strong and confident, some say it's because they're timid and unsure, and some say it's because they're just plain stupid," answered Bobbie.

"And what do you say?" asked Stanley.

"I'd say you don't know what's in an egg till you crack it."

Irish decided this would be a better conversation without him and begged off to find a soft spot to sleep.

"Well, mum. While your trying to crack this hard-boiled young yank here, I think I'll just rest me old bones. As difficult as that may be, considering some sly bugger went and snatched all me bolu. A heartless deed. A heartless deed indeed," he sighed as he rose and departed.

"You know, I certainly didn't expect to find things this exciting when I volunteered to come ashore," Bobbie told Stanley.

"I'd say you've handled it quite well so far, all but the dynamite that is."

"Are you saying I can't blow things up."

"Oh no. You can certainly do that. Opened up the whole side of the mountain," laughed Stanley. "You're, um… quite explosive. In a nice way, I mean."

"But I can't seem to open you up, mate. So maybe a well placed stick of dynamite…"

"No no," smiled Stanley. "I surrender. I'll talk."

"All right then. Let's start with this. What's a level headed yank like you doing makin' billy tea over a fire like some swagman and chasing pipe dreams on the other side of the world?"

"Funny you should say that, pipe dreams I mean. That's what my father called it. But I don't really have an answer just… a feeling. Like it was something I had to do and there were no excuses not to."

"I've been told you were born to fortune. Makes it a little hard to figure why you'd go swinging at windmills."

"Now who would tell you a thing like that?" asked Stanley.

"Why Barto of course," laughed Bobbie. "His exact words were, 'You have more money than brains and if it weren't for him you'd be lost in an affluent sea of decadence'."

"Bart said that?" laughed Stanley. "When?"

"Just before he asked me if I had ever been a Turkish belly dancer. We had a bit of a chinwag on the trail. He thinks a lot of you, you know."

"Bart has a way of seeing things from a unique perspective. Said something to me once," laughed Stanley. "He said, everybody is born with a bare ass, bare feet, a bare brain, and barely gives a damn about either one at the time, so why start now."

"Well, I suppose you could say that's a right weighty thought. He really is a genius isn't he?"

"Yeah, I guess he is at that... in his own sort of way. But don't be deceived. Under all that village idiot there's something special and profound. I know, I've seen it. Some day he's going to make a damn good lawyer."

"So he's just a bit of a comedian, then," said Bobbie.

"Yep, that's about it. His way of coping, you know?"

"And you?"

"Me?"

"You're the only bloke I'm talking to."

"I get the feeling I'm being interviewed for future concerns. You wouldn't be one of those gold diggers now would you?" asked Stanley.

"Nope. Just trying to crack an egg. Can't blame me if that egg happened to be laid by a golden goose now can ya?"

They were interrupted by a burst of laughter rising from around the other fire. Bobbie and Stanley looked over to see Monkey again harassing Bart.

What they didn't see beyond the glow of the fire and off in the shadows of the nearby forest was the strange and grossly painted face hiding in the darkness, watching, studying and waiting.

chapter 17

At the very first stream of daylight the exploratory team began loading themselves up for a deeper probe into the mountain. Their initial venture into the cave revealed that it extended far into the mountain but how far was an uncertainty. Stanley, Chrisfield, Big Tiny, Kicker, Edward and Lewis all donned packs containing torches, rope, tools, varied essentials and of course ammunition. Even in a cave, they decided that on this island they should be prepared for surprises. The other members of the expedition would remain outside the mountain to more develop the campsite and foray for food.

Chrisfield led the six-man team into the dark unknown, taking the only obvious route that always seemed to gradually descend. They had ventured about a full mile when they came to a chasm spanned by a narrow natural bridge. Chrisfield paused, looked back to Stanley and the others who all nodded approval, then he continued. While crossing the bridge Stanley looked down just a Chrisfield's careful footing met and pushed a loose stone over the side. He watched as the stone seemed to fall endlessly into the darkness to finally crack on impact with the bottom. None of them cared to calculate the distance to the bottom, knowing immediately that whatever the accuracy or conclusion of their calculations, the end total figured to be fatal should they happen to fall. They continued across carefully where they reached a ledge on the other side that presented the dilemma of proceeding in two different directions. Chrisfield moved his torch along the wall until he found a marking. It was a simple arrow about a foot long pointing to his left.

"Here's another one," he announced and continued on along the ledge.

The arrow was the third they had seen, the first nearer the mouth of the cave directing them in and including the initials J M.

The ledge curved around the wall then widened where they discovered a small subterranean river and waterfall. On the wall they found another arrow pointing to the falls.

"There's nowhere else to go except through those falls," observed Stanley. "We'll have to cover the torches to keep them dry. I'll go first, then relight mine on the other side. The rest of you can use my light as a guide to get through."

Stanley snubbed his torch out in the ground, removed his pack and jammed the torch into it. He then turned the pack upside down and made his way quickly through the waterfall. The five remaining men waited until they finally saw a flicker of light through the glistening water then one at a time repeated Stanley's actions with their torches and passed through the falls. Chrisfield was the last, wisely deciding to leave his torch mounted and burning on that side of the falls to guide them back.

When Chrisfield came through the cascading water he followed the light to a small passage to emerge into a huge cavern that expanded to various levels in all directions. He wiped the water from his face and looked about to find everyone except Stanley.

"Where's Stanley?" he asked.

"Don't know," answered Big Tiny. "Just the torch was here when we came through. Just the torch... and that."

Big Tiny pointed behind Chrisfield and held his torch up to offer a better lit view. Chrisfield turned to find a skeletal corpse lying against the cavern wall.

"I'd say he's been here a while," injected Kicker.

"Yeah, 'bout forty-five years according to that old sailor," responded Chrisfield as he inspected the remains. He then stood and looked out over the huge cavern and called out, "Stan! Stanley!"

Receiving no answer, he called again, "Wellington!"

"Here!" Stanley's voice echoed from far down and across the grotto.

They looked down in the distance to see a dim light.

"To your left. Come down to your left," instructed Stanley.

They moved off and descended into the cavern. As they did, Chrisfield gave an uneasy parting glance at the corpse.

The flickering light of their torches played off the minerals in the uneven walls and dome of the huge grotto, seemingly expanding it even more and giving it the appearance of an unnatural cathedral. When they reached the base of their downward trek, Stanley came out from around an outcropping with an old but still functioning oil lamp.

"Come here. Look at this," he said excitedly.

He led them around and into a chamber where they found scattered about were various pieces of old equipment and tools and the additional skeletal remains of seven men.

"It must be some of the crew of the Saint Jane," said Stanley.

"Yeah, we just met the doorman upstairs," said Lewis.

They moved about the chamber inspecting the bodies.

"Hey, this guy... I think this guy killed himself," observed Edward.

The corpse in question lay still holding the old navy Colt revolver used to blow away part of his head. Edward carefully lifted away the old pistol and opened it. It was empty except for a single spent cartridge.

"Yeah, so did this one. The hard way," said Stanley.

The corpse referred to by Stanley was in a kneeling position against the cavern wall, still holding the knife he shoved into his own heart.

"What in God's name would make them do that?" asked Lewis.

"It sure as hell wasn't money," answered Chrisfield.

He was kneeling next to another corpse holding a canvas sea bag. He turned it up and emptied out a pile of diamonds in the ruff.

"Diamonds," observed Chrisfield.

They all gathered around, picking up the stones, which were, as the old sailor said, big as your fist. They held them to the light and turned them about, surprised at their rough appearance. Chrisfield moved away and looked around the chamber.

"This chamber isn't natural. It was dug out. Probably by them," he observed.

Stanley looked down curiously at one of the dead sailors and noticed he held a pistol in one hand and a book in the other. He retrieved the book and examined it closely.

"What's that you've got there?" asked Edward, bringing his light closer to assist in its inspection.

"A Bible. And it's been written in," replied Stanley,

flipping through the book to the final written entry. "Listen to this," he called to the others, and then read the written entry from the book. "This was written on December 25th, 1889. All are dead save we seven. The Saint Jane is lost. No escape. No hope. Oh how I long for the freedom of the sea. Not even in God's words can I now find comfort for only God could have created such a curse as that great unearthly beast. What comfort is left us now on this our final Noel but the peace of death itself. I curse the greed that brought us to this place and resolve myself to die by my own hand. I die unforgiven yet it is far better than…"

"Than what?" asked Lewis.

"That's it. It ends there."

They stood in silence until Big Tiny spoke.

"We should bury them."

"Yes," agreed Stanley. "We'll take them out when we come back with the others."

Chrisfield glanced curiously at the cavern wall then walked over and inspected it more closely with his torchlight.

"Here. Give me more light over here."

Lewis and Stanley joined him with another torch. Chrisfield handed his torch to Stanley, pulled a pickax from his pack and tossed the pack to the ground. He rubbed his hands on the cavern wall to feel the place he was studying then stood back and struck it with the pickax. He struck it again and again until finally a large chunk of rock broke away. He retrieved it then chipped at it until it separated and a large stone the size of a grapefruit fell into his hand. They all stared as he held it up into the light.

"My God," he exclaimed. "It's... it's a single stone. A single... diamond."

"That dirty rock's a diamond?" asked Big Tiny.

"In the rough, Tiny. Like a beautiful princess cursed and hidden in the guise of a horny toad," laughed Chrisfield.

"Maybe you should kiss it then and see what happens," suggest his big friend.

Chrisfield kissed the stone then tossed it to Big Tiny.

"Hey, I could buy a new car with this?" suggested Big Tiny.

"No, you could buy a thousand new cars with that, Tiny," Answered Stanley with a smile. "Hell man, you could buy a small country."

They all laughed and started passing the stone around like a rugby ball. Chrisfield went back to inspecting the wall, running his hands over stone after stone. Stanley laughed then looked down to the dead sailors about the chamber and wondered. Suddenly a voice echoed throughout the grotto.

"Wellington! Chrisfield!" the voice echoed.

They all paused and listened closely. The desperate voice called out again.

"Wellington! Anybody! Help!"

They quickly exited the chamber into the grotto and looked up to discover James kneeling and waiving a torch high above at the caverns entrance.

"Here! We're down here!" returned Stanley.

James fell forward; losing his torch that spiraled down into the expansive grotto. Seeing this, the six men rushed up the side of the cavern to find him exhausted and barely conscious, bleeding from the head, shirt torn and holding a bleeding arm. He fell to his knees and collapsed. Big Tiny lifted him away from the edge of the grotto and pulled him to a more comfortable resting place.

"James! James! What happened," inquired Stanley.

Chrisfield began checking his wounds.

"James," Stanley repeated.

"Out of the jungle," James struggled to explain. "Everywhere. We didn't have time... Dead... Oscar and one of the Captain's men, dead. We couldn't..."

James tried again to speak then fell back unconscious in Chrisfield's arms. Stanley rose, dropped his gear except for his weapons, then wrapped a torch in preparation to return through the waterfall.

"What the hell happened out there?" asked Edward.

"I don't know but we better get there fast," answered Stanley.

"What about James here?" asked Chrisfield.

"You stay here with him," he instructed Chrisfield. "Do what you can. We'll come back for you."

The others followed Stanley's lead and all headed for the passage that led to the falls.

chapter 18

Stanley burst through the wall of water, quickly unwrapped his torch and finding the still burning light left by Chrisfield, retrieved and used it to light his own. Splashing through the falls behind him came Big Tiny followed by the others. Before Big Tiny could even wipe the water from his face Stanley shoved a torch into his hand and started off back through the cave. Disregarding all safety, he ran along the ledge to the natural bridge and darted across. Behind him followed Edward who in his haste slipped, fell and started to roll off into the abyss below. Big Tiny dove, dropping his torch but catching Edward by one hand just as he slid over the side. Looking down as he hung precariously, alive only by the strength and will of his oversized friend, he witnessed the torch falling endlessly until it crashed into a burst of sparks. Big Tiny had little to nothing to hold on to and only kept the both of them from falling by lying spread eagle across the narrow stone arch. As big and as strong as he was, he was quickly beginning to give in to the strain of holding on to Edward without any way of assisting him further. Stanley, who had moved on ahead finally returned after realizing he was alone. He planted his torch and dove across the narrow bridge and grabbed Edward's free hand. When the others arrived they assisted all three to safety.

"Are you alright?" asked Stanley of Edward.

"Yeah, but I think my arms are a little longer than they used to be."

"Okay then," nodded Stanley. "Come on. Let's go," he said as he jumped up, grabbed his torchlight and sprinted off.

They moved through the cave as fast as their limited light would permit, pausing only for a few seconds at a time to confirm their direction. When they finally saw daylight in the distance they stopped, dropped the torches and pulled their weapons. Stanley motioned quietly for Big Tiny and another to move to the opposite side of the cave then they all moved forward cautiously, weapons extended. They paused at the final turn until Stanley signaled, then rushed into the light surprised to discover a stack of rocks and wood debris forming a barricade to the outside. Positioned behind it was Captain Buckmaster nursing a wounded leg but still clutching a rifle. There was also one of the Captain's crew, four of the rugby boys and Irish. They were all slightly wounded but remained vigilant behind their hastily constructed wall. Near them lay the brutally battered bodies of Oscar and a Crimson Glory crewman.

They stared in disbelief as they emerged from the cave entrance, their eyes settling quietly on their dead comrades.

"What happened here?" asked Stanley.

"Natives," answered the Captain.

"From the village?"

"No. They were different, all painted up, wild. Hundreds of them," said Captain Buckmaster while pointing out past the barrier.

Stanley looked over to discover the bodies of dead natives strewn everywhere, evidence of a fierce fight in which their modern weapons obviously did the lion's share of damage. He then looked back around to the survivors behind the barrier.

"Where's Bart? And where's…"

"Captured… I think. We looked and couldn't find them. Natives must have taken them. Bart, Jonesy, three of your other boys…"

"And Bobbie?" Stanley asked.

"She went to the river with Monkey to…" the Captain cringed with pain, then continued. "…to get some water before the attack. I don't know where she is now."

Big Tiny came and kneeled next to the Captain and began inspecting and treating his wounds.

"What about the boy?" he asked.

"I don't know. It all happened so fast."

Suddenly they heard a noise at the edge of the jungle and everyone jumped to a defensive position behind the barricade. They readied their weapons and waited, heard the sound again then pointed the weapons with nervous trigger fingers to the area of the sound. The brush moved and their fingers tightened on the triggers.

"Hello! Is… anybody there?" came Bobbie as she and Monkey emerged from the bush.

Everyone relaxed.

Immediately upon seeing the dead natives, Monkey began to get antsy, showing some teeth and discharging a low growl. Stanley jumped over the barricade and Bobbie ran to meet him. The others joined them.

"Are you alright?" asked a much concerned Stanley.

Bobbie nodded a yes, "What happened here? I heard shots."

"We had visitors," answered Irish.

Bobbie looked around and seeing the carnage, began to take a mental accounting of who was present. "Where's Bart? And Jonesy and…"

"No time to waste," interrupted Stanley. "We have to go after them. Quick, get the weapons and ammo." He instructed the others then looked back to Captain Buckmaster, "Captain, Chrisfield is back in the cave attending to James. Get them and the other wounded and make your way down the river. You can signal the ship when you reach the shore."

Bobbie turned to Irish, "Where's…"

"They took 'em, mum. And God only knows what they'll do to 'em."

Bobbie marched over and snatched up an available Thompson machine gun. She was quickly intercepted by Stanley.

"Where do you think you're going?"

"With or without you, mate. End of discussion."

Just then Monkey lumbered up and looked into the cave. She looked around outside then back into the cave until she realized Bart was missing. She then looked at the dead natives, put it all together in her mind and let out a roar of protest.

Bobbie looked to Monkey then to Stanley, "Don't worry I've got backup. And she's pissed."

"Don't forget your dynamite." smiled Stanley. He then turned to Irish, "Irish, what's the count for our side?"

"I count eleven hardy souls, Gov, four Thompsons, five repeaters, fourteen forty-fives, a flame thrower, Big Tiny on the stove pipe, one elephant puncher and… um, the lady cook with her bang sticks."

Monkey sprinted to the edge of the jungle, stopped, turned back to the group and gave a quick growl then started dancing like a hound dog hot for some action. Bobbie slung on a bandoleer of ammo, threw on a pack full of dynamite and grabbed the Thompson.

"You heard the lady," she said, referring to Monkey. "Let's go."

chapter 19

The village was set against surrounding high protective cliffs closed in on the only open side by an exceptionally high man made wall. It was much like the village on the other side of the island except the structures and people were more clustered due to less available space within their protective canyon. The native community was hopping, to say the least, with throbbing drums and an insanely erratic witch doctor zig zagging about from group to group, raising hell in an effort to rouse their spirits. The crazed and wildly painted devilish natives, who, judging from the many heads mounted on polls about their huts, possessed an unquenchable appetite for fine human cuisine and needed little encouragement. It had been a good day because they had killed and been killed and even brought home the bacon in the form of prisoners.

In the center of the village and the focal point of all the high anxiety antics were Bart, Jonesy, and the three rugby boys, stripped to the waist, cut and bruised and tied with their hands above their heads to poles. Their heads hung down as they labored to stay conscious, watching and hoping their fate would not be the obvious. The wild and wide eyed witch doctor danced, circled a large fire and man sized boiling caldron then struck the large pot with his juju stick. He then danced over to Bart and whacked him across the chest. Bart flinched with pain as the witch doctor circled the caldron again and returned to strike him once more. Again he circled, coming around to strike one of the rugby boys. It was tenderizing time.

Two fat native mamas, the designated cooks for the evening, approached Jonesy and started poking him with their fingers, laughing, then pinched his tit. Jonesy painfully raised his head and one of the mamas offered up a large toothless smile of anticipation. About that time the witch doctor made another round and whacked Jonesy across the chest, causing the toothless fat mama to whirl quickly and whack the witch doctor in return. Ranting and raving, the scrawny wiry witch doctor grew angry, turned and struck one of the rugby boys exceptionally hard, further raising the ire of the toothless fat mama who gave the crazed medicine man hell and chased him off.

From a nearby hut emerged the carnivorous Chief who was immediately approached by the screaming witch doctor expressing his grievances and taking refuge from the pursuing fat mama cook. The Chief slapped the little man down like an annoying dog and left him to the mercy of the big woman who immediately began kicking him. The Chief then walked over and inspected his captives, taking particular interest in Bart. He pulled out a very large and serious knife and placed it under his chin, raising his head. A dazed and expressionless Bart looked into the Chief's eyes. After inspecting his fair skin and freckles with intense curiosity the Chief brought the knife away and Bart's head dropped heavily. The Chief then reached up and cut off a hand full of blond hair, studied it, sniffed it and walked away.

If the sound had included a twelve-cylinder diesel engine and clanking metal it could have passed for a rampaging army tank tearing through the jungle but it was instead Monkey who was wasting no time cutting a beeline for the cannibal village. Running at a desperate pace to keep up behind her was Bobbie, Stanley and the others with jungle growth slapping them about the face and debris from Monkey's wake falling all around. Suddenly they reached a broad field that expanded into open rolling hills. Monkey paused only momentarily then sprinted off across the field.

"Monkey stop!" called Bobbie.

Monkey stopped and turned. The rest of the party

paused, huffing and puffing to catch their wind. Monkey watched impatiently as Stanley searched the ground for signs and tracks. Then Stanley grew excited as he ran over, discovered and snatched up Jonesy's hat.

"This way," he stated, holding up the hat. "Come on. This way."

They all continue at a quick pace following Stanley's lead, all but Monkey that is, who had other ideas altogether. She growled, shook her head, and they all stopped. She then shook her arms excitedly and started off in another direction.

"Monkey no. This way," called Stanley.

Monkey stopped, shook her head again and motioned with an arm for them to continue in her chosen direction.

"Maybe she knows a short cut," suggested Bobbie. "After all, it's her island."

"No," insisted Stanley. "I can see their trail. It's this way."

Stanley started off again in the direction of the trail only to suddenly find himself being swooped up by Monkey's large hand. Cradling him like a rugby ball, she took off across the field, leaving the rest behind.

"HEY!" cried Bobbie.

Monkey stopped.

"Give us a break, will ya," she pleaded.

Bobbie and the others then moved off to follow Monkey who waited impatiently for them to catch up then took off again.

It was near dusk when the group arrived at the edge

of some rugged mountains were they paused for a breather. Stanley was back on the ground now after giving in to Monkey's possibly better and definitely undisputable judgment.

"Stanley, we've got to rest," pleaded Bobbie.

Stanley looked to her with desperate eyes, determined to continue at all cost.

"Please," she pleaded again. Plopping down on the ground.

He reluctantly agreed with a simple nod and they all removed their gear and sat, pulling out canteens, drinking and washing the miles of dirty sweat from their faces. Even Monkey acquiesced, though she stood eagerly ready to continue. Stanley moved away from the others and sat alone placing his arms on his knees. He looked off into the sunset then dropped his face in his hands.

"He means a lot to you doesn't he."

He raised his head to find Bobbie sitting beside him.

"They all do."

"But Bart's special. A good friend. Like a brother."

"Yeah."

"Why?" asked Bobbie. "I mean, you've got a boat load of friends here. Why Bart?"

Stanley thought a moment then replied, "Because he's honest, uncomplicated, unpretentious. Everything I'm not, I suppose."

"He does kind of grow on you doesn't he?" smiled Bobbie.

"Yeah," chuckled Stanley who then grows solemn. "I brought them here. I killed them."

"No you didn't, mate. They came because they wanted to. To prove themselves and challenge life. Just like you. You men have been doing that for all time, right? I mean, that's the difference in the species isn't it. The difference between a monkey and a man."

"You're beginning to sound like Bart."

"I think I'll take that as a compliment," she laughed. "I think."

"And what about you? What are you trying to prove?" inquired Stanley in return.

"Not sure. That I can be as good a friend as your Barto and maybe learn as much as Jonesy… without sacrificing my dignity."

Stanley looked at her and touched her face.

"You have more dignity than any woman I've ever met," he said sincerely.

"You're not so bad yourself," she smiled affectionately. "For a Yank that is."

Suddenly, drifting through the darkening sky came the sound of distant drums. Stanley perked.

"Listen!"

The drums grew louder and Monkey grew uncomfortable, grunted displeasure and scowled. Stanley rose and turned to the boys who were already on their feet and donning their gear.

"That's it. Let's move," ordered Stanley.

The eleven would-be rescuers cautiously rounded a rocky outcropping at a trot with Monkey bringing up the rear. Stanley raised his hand and held them up when he saw the large wall; which closed in and secured the village, designed to protect them from the exceptionally large predators of the island. It was easily over sixty feet high, well over five hundred feet long and constructed of huge trees three deep with a series of torch lights across the top at about twenty foot intervals. A line of narrow steps for human use and entry to the village ascended the wall at each end appearing to be the only obvious entry. From the other side they could hear the drums and the occasional whoops and screams of celebrating natives. Stanley looked from one end of the wall to the other, readied his rifle and started forward but was halted when Irish grabbed him by the arm.

"Hold on there, laddie. We can't just walk in there like a bunch of uninvited in-laws."

Irish looked and inspected the wall and the surrounding cliffs.

"This is going to take a little old fashioned Irish finesse," he said as he brought the group together and laid out a plan of attack. "We stay together in teams of two. Big Tiny, you and Kicker get on those rocks up there above the village. Use that stove pipe of yours so you can get the most for your money. Now, who's got the flame thrower?"

"Here," answered Bradley.

"Good. You stay with me, boyo, he said as he turned

to Stanley and the others. "Stanley, you and three others get over the wall on the far end there. I'll take the rest with me over the wall on this end. Team up and stay together. Missy, you better stay with me."

"Nope," Bobbie said flatly.

They all looked at Bobbie, confused.

"Alright. You go with Stanley then."

"Nope," repeated Bobbie.

"Now this is no time for arguing, mum."

She smiled and pulled out a few sticks of dynamite, "I'm going in the front door."

When Monkey saw the dynamite she cringed and her hands immediately went to her butt.

"Bobbie, there is no front door," said Stanley.

"Not yet," she smiled.

"Alright then, I'll go with you."

"Nope."

Stanley looked at Bobbie, exasperated, "Now listen…"

"It's alright. I'm in good hands," she interrupted, pointing a thumb up to Monkey. She then started shoving sticks of dynamite in her shirt and trousers.

Stanley shook his head in defeat, "Are all the women in Australia like you?"

"Now if I answer that all you boys are likely to leave me here and head that little boat of yours down under."

"Not likely," said Stanley.

"Hey Big Tiny, got a cigar?" she asked.

Big Tiny looked to Bobbie confused, questioning the

request.

"To light the fuses," she explained.

"Oh. Right," he replied and handed her a cigar, which she promptly popped between her teeth. He then struck a match and lit her up, amazed at how easily she took to the predominantly male habit.

"Alright then. That's our signal. When Bobbie blows the wall, we attack," announced Irish.

With that final point of instruction they separated into groups, locking and loading their weapons. Big Tiny and Kicker moved off to ascend the end of the wall and on up to the rocky ledges overlooking the village. While Irish prepared himself he looked to Stanley with a broad smile and offered one of his impromptu half-ass limericks.

"There once was a boy who called himself Stan that went off in search of a far away land. Upon it he found things both great and profound, and returned… one hell of a man."

Stanley looked to Irish and smiled as he slung his rifle over his shoulder and checked his pistols, "You know Irish, I've often wondered about…"

"Alright mates," said Irish, cutting him off as if he knew what he was about to say. "Let's go make a house call."

He and his group start to move off for the wall then he looked back to Stanley, "Hey boyo. You tell your grandfather… you tell that old bastard he was right. You tell him I said so," He said then turned and ran off with the others.

Stanley stood briefly confused then he too turned and moved off with his group for the far end of the wall. They went rapidly through the shadows along the base of the wall, all the while watching the top for any natives that might be posted at guard. Fortunately they had all gone to dinner, leaving the wall abandoned.

Bobbie and Monkey now stood alone.

"Well girl. Looks like we're stuck in the kitchen again."

Monkey watched the others depart with a sigh of concern and a sense of danger.

chapter 20

The natives of the village were out in the hundreds now, dancing and mingling around their fires and torchlights, moving about in a frenzy of celebration and preparation of their upcoming feast. They pounded on drums along with a myriad of other racket making instruments almost as though they were intoxicated or high on some form of drug. As they celebrated they moved ever closer to the meal of honor captives still bound to the post.

On a ledge above the village, Big Tiny and Kicker reached an advantageous spot and looked down.

"Damn Tiny, there's hundreds of them," observed Kicker.

Big Tiny popped in a fresh cigar, chewed and

grimaced, "Not for long there isn't."

He readied the bazooka and positioned himself securely on the ledge while Kicker unpacked the ammo and lined it up on the ground next to him.

Stanley and his assault team came over the crest of the wall to discover the sight of the village for the first time. Stanley looked about until he found the descending steps on the opposite side of the wall, pointed them out to the others then instructed them to hold there until they received the signal. As he surveyed the village he saw Bart, Jonesy and the other captives hanging helplessly on the post.

"They're alive. They're still alive!"

Irish and his men came over the wall to find a similar set of narrow steps and the same disturbing sight of hundreds of crazed natives. Irish looked into the village then across and down the long line of dim torches to the other end of the wall in an effort to see Stanley. If they were there they were hidden in the darkness thought Irish, and he knew they were there waiting for Bobbie's signal, just as he would be. He leaned back over the wall and looked down to Bobbie, giving her the okay sign. A cigar puffing Bobbie caught his signal, acknowledged, then readied her Thompson and moved off in a careful crouch through the shadows beneath the wall. Monkey followed in much the same manner though there wasn't nearly enough shadow to hide her near thirty-foot presence. When they reached the approximate center of the wall Bobbie stopped, looked about and turned to

Monkey.

"Okay, mate. Time to do some cookin'," she said as she began to pull out a few sticks of dynamite.

The sight of the explosives immediately made Monkey uncomfortable and she began to go into a nervous dance of concern.

"Shush. Settle down. It's just a little dynamite," whispered Bobbie.

Monkey grew more agitated by the second, patting her wounded ass. She began sighing like a child desperate to relieve itself but having no restroom in sight.

"Will you knock it off? They're going to hear you," pleaded Bobbie as she withdrew another stick of explosive and began lashing them all together.

Monkey continued scooting nervously back and forth, then jumped and grabbed the top of the wall, pulled herself up enough to peek over into the village and immediately caught sight of Bart and the others at the mercy of their captors. Just then the crazy ass witch doctor danced around and struck Bart mercilessly with his juju stick causing him to cry out in pain. Witnessing this, Monkey immediately goes... well, *ape-shit,* and lets out a tremendous angry ROAR of displeasure that echoed off the canyon walls and through the village with incredible magnitude. The entire native population of the village came to a standstill, turned and looked to the wall.

Bart raised his head and strained to force a smile

through his pain. "Monkey. You bastards are in for it now," he strained to say, then passed out.

The wiry little witch doctor unwisely looked to the great wall and raising his juju stick in the air screamed defiantly in return, angering Monkey even more. Monkey let out another tremendous reverberating ROAR. She dropped to the ground, picked up Bobbie and set her aside, moved back then roared again as she charged and rammed the wall. The formidable structure shook, sending dirt, dust, torches and years of old growth careening to the ground. Monkey charged again. This time the wall began to give and fell partially inward. Both Irish and Stanley's men atop each end of the wall watched Monkey in awe while they held tight to whatever they could in an effort not to be thrown by the earthquake like vibrations. On the ground Bobbie stood in total amazement at Monkey's power and resolve. She moved back to safety as she watched the great gorilla crank up for another attack. Monkey roared, charged and crashed again into the wall with unbelievable force.

Inside the village the hundreds of natives stared in disbelief as their long enduring massive wall crashed inward and through it charged a mass of roaring frightening terror. Monkey angrily hauled one of the huge tree trunks which were part of the now destroyed wall up over her head and hurled it into the village, destroying half a dozen huts and a number of fleeing natives. At the same time Big Tiny fired his bazooka, sending a round rocketing into the largest group of natives, resulting in bodies and body parts flying in all directions. Many of the natives scattered in the confusion until Big Chief Carnivore began to bark orders, sending them to retrieve their weapons. Another bazooka round blew up a nearby hootch and the battle was on.

Stanley's team was the first to fire as they charged down the steps toward the village. From the other end of the wall on the other side of the village Irish and company began the same, firing and yelling, confusing the natives even more. The scurrying natives were dropping everywhere within the sight and range of the Crimson Glory rescuers. Then, through the rubble of the destroyed portion of the wall entered a cigar toking Bobbie, the Thompson machine gun in one hand and a stick of dynamite in the other. When she walked through a roaring Monkey's legs she spied an oncoming rush of drug crazed natives, lit the short fused dynamite with the cigar and heaved. Monkey, seeing the dynamite, grew wide-eyed and immediately crouched and covered her head. The dynamite exploded and the unfortunate natives flew in all directions. Others turned and ran only to get caught in the crossfire of Irish and Stanley's attacks. After the violent explosion, Monkey peaked out, looked around and then checked her ass, which was to her relief still all there.

Big Chief Carnivore turned for the safety of his large hut just as Big Tiny and Kicker leveled it with another bazooka round sending the chief into a rage and a mad desire for vengeance. In his anger he ripped a spear from a passing native and headed for the prisoners that were tied and ready for roasting. His first choice for revenge was Bart. He moved in front of him, smiled sadistically and brought the spear to bear.

At that same moment Monkey looked to Bart and saw the Chief about to run him through. Stanley, rushing through the chaos saw the same thing and raised his rifle but before he could fire Monkey roared and raced across the village, knocking aside a hut and assorted natives. She swiftly reached down and swooped up the Chief, brought him face to face with her anger then let out a snarl and a tremendous angry ROAR! The Chief, screaming like a banshee, was thrown like a major league curve ball over the entire village to crash violently into the side of the rocky canyon wall. Turning back, Monkey caught a quick glimpse of the crazy ass village witch doctor taking refuge in a nearby hut. She ripped up the entire hut and threw it aside, roared her displeasure, snatched up the now screaming little juju jammer and jammed him head first into the large boiling caldron. Bart began to come around and looked up to Monkey, smiled, then passed out again. Monkey stayed near the captives, protecting them by swatting away any natives which ran near as though they were nothing more than pesky insects. Nearby the rescuers began closing in on the village, firing continuously.

Irish grabbed Bradley with the flamethrower, "Burn the huts!" he yelled as he pushed him forward. "Put the fear o' the devil himself in 'em me boyo!"

Bradley approached a hut, aimed the flamethrower and squeezed the trigger but nothing happened. He shook it, pulled the trigger again... nothing, and again with no results. Irish ran up and pulled the flamethrower pack off Bradley's back.

"Forget it! No time!" he yelled.

Then, like an Olympic hammer thrower, he heaved the entire flame throwing contraption into an onrushing crowd of crazed natives, drew his .45, shot and triggered a massive jelly bomb of an explosion which sent crispy burning natives in all directions.

"Ha ha!" laughed a wild-eyed Irish. "Never underestimate the Irish, you bastard buggers! It'll come 'round to bite ya on the arse every time."

Stanley was working his way to the captives, firing his rifle at every turn. When it ran empty he reached for more ammo and discovered he was out. He quickly tossed the rifle and pulled out his two .45s and continued firing, knowing and worrying that the same would happen to the others soon.

On their advantageous perch up above the village Big Tiny watched with keen interest then quickly rose.

"Come on!" he yelled to Kicker.

"But we've got more rounds."

"Bring 'em," yelled Big Tiny. "I gotta' find the kid!"

Kicker quickly gathered up the few remaining bazooka rounds and they both began carefully descending the rocky terrain down to the village.

Bobbie linked up with the boys, offered them a smile and lit two sticks of dynamite.

"Hey, Irish!" she yelled over.

Irish turned just in time to catch a stick of sizzling lit dynamite then he and Bobbie tossed them simultaneously into a large group the charging natives. The double whammy from Bobbie's never before seen explosive magic was the last thing most of them would ever see and the more fortunate lay stunned and unconscious. Irish again let out a laugh but just as he did a native rushed him with a spear. He managed to deflect the spear only to be pierced with the same native's long knife. Irish kicked the native in the groin then shot him twice with his .45. Holding his wound, he turned to Bobbie.

"Too close for any more of them bang sticks, mum."

Bobbie nodded agreement and ripped loose with the Thompson, taking out at least half a dozen of the killer cannibals with the first burst of rounds. Then seemingly from nowhere came the screaming toothless fat mamma with a club hell bent on splitting Bobbies head. Bobbie whirled with a right cross, sending the big woman horizontal and knocking her out cold.

Through the smoke and screams and chaos Stanley finally managed to reach Bart.

"Bart! Bart!" he yelled. "Come on man, talk to me."

Bart remained silent and unconscious while Stanley cut him free and laid him on the ground then quickly went to the others and did the same. Monkey hovered over Bart, shielding him, snatching, tossing and swatting away natives. A good part of the village was now burning and though many of the natives had been turned into casualties there were many more which kept coming. Irish, Bobbie and the others, some wounded, were fighting their way into a protective ring around Stanley and the captives.

"We're running out of ammo!" Irish called to Stanley. "There's too damn many of 'em!"

When Stanley looked to Irish, he saw a group of natives charging up behind him.

"Behind you!" he warned.

Irish turned, firing, joined by Bobbie and the natives went down but others advanced from behind a nearby hut. Suddenly a bazooka round rocketed just over Irish's shoulder and the hut and natives were taken out by the resulting explosion. A surprised Irish turned to find Big Tiny and Kicker. Big Tiny looked around desperately.

"Where's the kid?" he yelled to Irish.

Irish had no answer and he quickly looked to the others who also came up blank.

"I'm out of ammo!" cried Mule.

"Same here!" echoed Bradley.

Those with ammunition continued firing. Stanley reloaded and tossed his .45 to Mule who wasted no time using it. With the shortage of ammunition their firing now became more selective. The natives continued to fall then they began backing off into the village to regroup. The rescuers stood there in the sudden silence, huffing and puffing, tired and fearful. Some began checking their wounds.

"That's it then," said Mule. "We don't have enough ammo to fight our way out of here."

The natives began to slowly filter their way out of the village, determined to make a final effective and victorious charge.

"Tiny, you got any juice left in that thing," asked Bobbie.

"One more round, Ma'am," replied Big Tiny, chewing nervously on his still unlit cigar.

Bobbie pulled out her remaining sticks of dynamite and passed them around, "Guess we all go out with a bang, mates."

Stanley joined the circle, reloading his .45 and turning to Irish, "So Irish. Are you going to tell me how you happen to know my grandfather?"

Irish, also reloading his weapon, laughed hardily, "You're name might be English, laddie, but you're as Irish as me own mum."

"What?"

"Oh hell, boyo. I'm your uncle. In a non-conjugal sort of way."

Stanley stared, confused, then saw the approaching natives. Monkey saw them as well and let loose with a threatening roar! Her roar no longer impressed the natives however, who had become either stupid or stoned during their pre-feast festivities. The natives cautiously approached, spreading out their number and raising their weapons. The rescuers tensed and the few who had ammunition raised their weapons as well.

Big Tiny lined up his sights on a particularly nasty looking native who was now leading their remaining force of nearly two hundred approaching cannibals.

"This one's for you, big man," he said as he shifted his cigar.

Bobbie went to the fire burning under the big black caldron from which protruded the legs of the now well done wiry little witch doctor. She was about to light the fuse of a stick of dynamite when suddenly from behind them by the destroyed wall, came the thunderous declaration of another native chief.

"BOLUUUUUU!"

They quickly turned to discover big Chief Shit Head and hundreds of his Bolu Boys, all dressed, painted and loaded for bear. Next to Chief Shit Head stood Boy wearing Big Tiny's pack and sporting a broad smile. Chief Shit Head shoved the boy aside to safety, raised his spear and charged, followed by the entire Bolu Social Club with their hundreds of voices thundering out their war cry.

"BOLUUUUUU!"

The cannibals screamed a brief series of insults, shook their spears and long knives in contempt then turned and hauled ass, closely and mercilessly pursued by the bolu boys. The native clash was gruesome to say the least but welcomed by the Crimson Glory group who fell back, exhausted.

Bobbie and Stanley went to Bart and Jonesy. The

others cared for the other captives and their own wounds.

"Jonesy! Jonesy!" cried Bobbie as she raised him into her lap.

Jonesy slowly opened his eyes to Bobbie and forced a bit of a smile, "Nice of you to drop by... for dinner, ma'am."

Bobbie smiled with relief and began checking his wounds.

Big Tiny looked over to Boy who was still waiting obediently by the rubble of the old wall. He gave a whistle and the boy's smile grew as he ran to his newfound friends. Big Tiny smiled in return and tossed the boy up on his shoulders.

"Nice piece of work bringing in the cavalry like that, Little Bit," Big Tiny said to the boy.

"I bring you something else, Sailorman Tiny. I keep it from the bad people," said Boy as he reached into the pack, withdrew Big Tiny's rugby ball and handed it to him with a prideful smile of achievement.

"Keep it, champ. You earned it," said Big Tiny, handing it back to him.

Bart finally came around and looked up to Stanley, forcing as much as he could his signature shit-eating smile.

"You can pick the damndest places to take a cruise," he said, raising his hand to meet Stanley's.

"I'm inclined to agree with you, old man," answered Stanley. "And I think this particular outing is just about over."

"Good. I was getting a little bored here anyway," Bart chuckled painfully.

Monkey sat looking at Bart with near motherly affection when one of the cannibals lying nearby got up to run. She swatted him like a fly.

chapter 21

The sun shown brightly and a pleasant constant breeze flowed over the white sandy beach where they said their goodbyes. They were all cleaned up now and in better spirits with their wounds tended, fed and rested, and their dead buried. Nearby, the two launches from the Crimson Glory sat loaded and waiting.

All about the beach the emotions ran high. The natives of Monkey Island, as the visitors had come to call it, had taken quite a shine to the strange crew and the rugby boys from old Princeton. In like manner the once naively adventuresome young rugby boys had come to appreciate a native culture that had for so long been lost to the rest of the world. All this led to the informal farewells turning into an exchange of gifts and even promises to some day return.

"This is for big monsters. Dinosaurs," Big Tiny tried to explain to Chief Shit Head as he presented him with a gift of the bazooka. "Um… big lizards."

He looked to Boy for assistance in helping him through the language barrier.

"Sailorman Shit Head call them big pig fuckers. Grrrrr," explained Boy, making a motion like a dinosaur.

"Um… yeah. Big… pigs," said Big Tiny.

Nearby, Chrisfield was handing a Thompson machine gun to one of the bolu boys.

"This for killing bad coons," explained Chrisfield.

The bolu boy smiled and shook his head as though he understood completely, "Yes. Yes."

"This gun, pop pop pop bang bang bang. Kill all bad coons," Chrisfield explained further. "Then you can move back to the big city. Get civilized again. Build a bar and sell bolu."

"Pop pop bang bang. Boluuuuu!" smiled the bolu boy as he accepted the weapon.

"No no. No drink bolu when use pop pop bang bang," warned Chrisfield.

"Bolu. Pop pop bang bang," smiled the grateful native.

Further down the beach Jonesy passed by Irish as he was receiving the gift of a big jug of bolu.

"Whatcha' got there, Irish?" asked Jonesy.

"Bolu," smiled Irish. "And I got the recipe. I'm gonna' bottle this stuff and become a rich man. Think I'll call it, McGonegal's Finest."

"McGonegal?"

"My name, boyo," explained Irish, pointing a thumb to his chest. "Milton Byron McGonegal. At you service."

"Milton Byron," repeated Jonesy. "That figures."

"All loaded, Skipper!" One of the ship's crew yelled from the side of a launch.

The skipper stood with Bart, Stanley, and Bobbie who were saying their goodbyes to Monkey. He turned and headed for the launch at the call of the crewman.

"Time and tide waits for no man," said the Captain as he departed. "Oh… or no woman."

"I'm sorry, Monkey. We can't take you with us," said Bart.

Monkey moaned disappointment.

"You wouldn't like it anyway. It's cold and crowded and noisy. Indoor plumbing."

Monkey sighed, reached down with a finger and knocked Bart on his ass, offering a pitiful little chuckle.

Bart got up and continued, "Besides, you've got new friends now. Just… just don't drink any bolu and don't sit on anybody if you do, okay?"

Monkey sighed and plopped down, looking to Bobbie for a little female support.

"I know. They love ya then they leave ya. Comes with the territory girly," said Bobbie. "Ya gotta' stay strong."

Monkey sat and sniffed, rubbed her nose.

"Bart, time to go," reminded Stanley as he and Bobbie moved off to board the launch.

"Um, I want you to know I really appreciate what you did for me," Bart continued. "I mean you rally saved my ass more than once and I'll never forget it. Never."

Monkey sniffed.

"Maybe I'll come back to see you some day. Would you like that?" Bart asked of Monkey, hoping to cheer her up.

She sniffed with a slight nod of approval.

"Maybe I'll bring you something to play with. Like… like the Empire State Building or something."

Bart turned to see all the others were in the launches waiting. He turned back to Monkey. "I have to go now. So you go home, okay?" he said, pointing to the mountains. "You have to go home now."

Monkey reached down to knock him on his ass again but Bart moved away.

"No. No more play. Bart's going home and Monkey has to go home. Monkey… has to go home."

Bart turned and walked away. At the launch he turned and looked back to see Monkey express a long emotional sigh.

As the launches were rowed toward the ship the natives of the Bolu tribe drifted slowly back into the nearby jungle. In one launch were Stanley, Bart, Bobbie, the Captain, Chrisfield, Stinky, and a few others. Each rowed in sad silence until Stinky looked to Stanley with the question many of them had wanted to ask.

"What about the diamonds?"

"What about 'em?" answered Stanley. "Not eager to shed any more blood just for riches."

"Oh, you mean this," said Chrisfield.

They all looked to find Chrisfield smiling and holding the grapefruit size stone he had dug from the cavern wall. He then reached down under his seat and lifted a heavy pack.

"And these."

Opening the pack he displayed the diamonds they found in the cavern with the dead crew of the Saint Jane.

"Well young Wellington. It appears your venture wasn't a bust after all," observed Captain Buckmaster.

"Especially if you include the other six bags," added Chrisfield.

"Bags?" asked Stanley.

"Of diamonds," continued Chrisfield. "On the other boat. A gift from Chief Shit Head actually. It seems they were left behind by the old sailor when he hurried off the island. The Chief had no use for them."

"I guess there's enough to go around, then," smiled Stanley.

"More than enough," answered Chrisfield. "But the chief threw in a catch."

"A catch?" asked Bobbie.

Chrisfield nodded over to the other launch where they looked and saw sitting on Big Tiny's shoulders as he rowed, the son of the son of Sailorman Shit Head,

Boy.

"We're supposed to fill the little buggers head with civilized bull shit and then send him home to take over the island. If we can correct his English enough to take him out in public, that is."

They all laughed then looked back to the beach where Monkey was making her way along the shore, looking out to the boats, grunting and throwing out her hand in appeal.

"I feel like shit," said an unhappy Bart. "Worse, like my dog died in the worst way, run over by a car full of nuns."

Everyone had boarded the Crimson Glory and the crew were raising and securing the launches when Bart, Stanley and Bobbie where joined by Big Tiny and Boy to give the island a final farewell look. Across the water on the beach Monkey had come to a wide place on the sand where she stopped, looked out to the ship and let out a loud cry of anguish which seemed to carry across the surface and into the sails. Bart lowered his head and turned away.

"Up anchor!" called out Captain Buckmaster.

"Aye, Skipper."

"First Mate, give her some sail! Give her all we've got! We sail for home!"

"Aye Capt'n," acknowledged the First Mate. "Full sail it be."

While the crew busied themselves about the ship,

Bobbie moved closer to Stanley's side.

"You'll have quite a story to tell back in America," she said.

Stanley nodded agreement.

"But I think Bart is right."

"Right? About what?"

"That you have a serious lack of imagination. And I think you're going to need someone with a lot of flair who does have some imagination to help you tell that story."

"Is that right," replied Stanley, turning to face her. "Wouldn't have someone special in mind would you."

"I might," she smiled. "But it's a long story. Might take a while. So I think I might be needing to stop off in Sydney and take care of some business first."

"Oh no. You're not planning to blow up some more planes are you?" asked Stanley.

"Nah. Nothing so trivial. Think I'll just let the law deal with those blokes. I just need to stop off for a bit of accounting. You see, my father didn't just fly planes he also built them. About ten million dollars worth of planes a year actually."

Stanley smiled, the ship's bell sounded and they came together in a lingering kiss until they were suddenly interrupted by the cries of an excited Boy.

"Myuko! Sailormans quick look see!" called out Boy. "Myuko!"

On deck and high in the rigging crewmen stopped what they were doing and looked off to shore, speechless, dumbfounded, and awestruck. Everyone on deck paused and looked to the island. Bart was about to go below decks when he turned and looked back to the island as well. When he did his great signature shit-eating smile returned, spreading slowly over his face as he realized that everything now made sense. He rushed to the side of the ship for a better view.

Monkey sat on the beach sobbing and looking out to the ship when suddenly there came a tremendous BOOM! BOOM! BOOM! until eventually stepping up behind her came the two enormous legs and feet of another gorilla. The intrusion hardly phased Monkey who looked up then back to the Crimson Glory and sighed. A large gorilla hand reached down, Monkey took hold and was lifted easily off the ground and placed on the broad shoulders of her mother. They turned and headed into the jungle.

The entire ship's company stared in silent amazement until the silence was broken by Bart who burst into joyous laughter.

Monkey turned from her perch atop mother Myuko's shoulders for a final glance at the departing ship in majestic full sail. She let out a roaring farewell and Myuko joined in, giving off a roar so great it rocked the entire island.

about the author

A native of Annapolis, Maryland, award-winning Writer/Photographer Frank Mosco, after many years in Florida, now resides and writes in Virginia. The former broadcast and print journalist who has written and produced material for all forms of media now spends most of his time creating works of fiction that in his words, *"Can be just as strange as reality but far more convenient, and definitely more fun."*

Visit the author's web site at;
www.frankmosco.com